Elle of the Ball

Also by Elena Delle Donne

My Shot

HOOPS
Elle of the Ball

1

Elena Delle Donne

Simon & Schuster Books for Young Readers
New York   London   Toronto   Sydney   New Delhi

SIMON & SCHUSTER BOOKS FOR YOUNG READERS
An imprint of Simon & Schuster Children's Publishing Division
1230 Avenue of the Americas, New York, New York 10020
This book is a work of fiction. Any references to historical
events, real people, or real places are used fictitiously. Other
names, characters, places, and events are products of the author's
imagination, and any resemblance to actual events or places or
persons, living or dead, is entirely coincidental.
Text copyright © 2018 by Elena Delle Donne
Jacket illustration copyright © 2018 by Cassey Kuo
All rights reserved, including the right of reproduction in whole or
in part in any form.
SIMON & SCHUSTER BOOKS FOR YOUNG READERS
is a trademark of Simon & Schuster, Inc.
For information about special discounts for bulk purchases,
please contact Simon & Schuster Special Sales at 1-866-506-1949
or business@simonandschuster.com.
The Simon & Schuster Speakers Bureau can bring authors to your
live event. For more information or to book an event, contact the
Simon & Schuster Speakers Bureau at 1-866-248-3049 or visit our
website at www.simonspeakers.com.
Jacket design by Laurent Linn
Interior design by Hilary Zarycky
The text for this book was set in Minister.
Manufactured in the United States of America
0218 FFG
First Edition
2 4 6 8 10 9 7 5 3 1
CIP data for this book is available from the Library of Congress.
ISBN 978-1-5344-1231-6
ISBN 978-1-5344-1233-0 (eBook)

To Gia

Acknowledgments

I have a team of people that I would like to thank, and I fully recognize that I would not be where I am today without the support of my family and friends behind me.

Amanda, my wife and my best friend, you have given up and sacrificed so much to help me better my career (even being my off-season workout partner). Words cannot express how much you mean to me, and I am so excited that you are with me for life. We are a pretty unstoppable team.

Special thanks to my incredible parents, who have been with me since day one. Mom, thank you for being extremely honest, absolutely hilarious, and my ultimate role model for what strength looks like.

Dad, thank you for driving me all the way to Pennsylvania twice a week, attending every AAU tournament, and still traveling to lots of my WNBA games. You are my biggest fan.

To my older sister, Lizzie, thank you for helping me keep everything in perspective. You remind me that there is so much more to life, and that joys can come from anywhere—even something as simple as the wind or a perfectly cooked rib eye. You are the greatest gift to our family. And thanks to my big brother, Gene, for being able to make me laugh, especially through the lows, and for being my biggest cheerleader.

Wrigley, my greatest friend and Greatest Dane. Thanks for being my rock in Chicago and for attacking me with love every time I come home. Rasta, thanks for being the edge and sass in our home and for being the only one in our house who can keep Amanda in check.

Erin Kane and Alyssa Romano, thank you for helping me discover myself and for helping me find my voice. This wouldn't have happened without the greatest team behind me.

Thanks to my Octagon literary agent, Jennifer Keene, for all her great work on this project. Thanks to the all-stars at Simon & Schuster, including Liz Kossnar.

Thank you all.

Elle of the Ball

My Height Is Ruining My Life!

When you are tall for your age—not just a little tall, but extremely tall—there is one question that everybody asks you: "Do you play basketball?"

People had been asking me that question ever since third grade, when I was so tall that I looked like I belonged in sixth grade. It used to annoy me. Just because I was tall, I was supposed to like basketball? *And* automatically be good at it? It didn't seem fair. I was tall, so I was destined to play basketball, whether I liked it or not.

So I guess it's good that I actually ended up liking basketball. That's because of my brother, Jim. He's five years older than I am, and he's really into sports. In our house there was always some kind of game on TV, and so I grew up watching Michael Jordan in the NBA and Sheryl Swoopes in the WNBA. We also had a basketball hoop in our driveway, so Jim taught me how to shoot, and when I got good at it we'd play against each other.

When I was in fifth grade, I joined the basketball team at school, and I'd been playing ever since. I'd been growing ever since, too. By the summer I was twelve years old, I'd shot up to six feet tall.

That's right. Six feet. In seventh grade, most people are around five feet tall. That made me taller than every single kid in my grade, including the boys, and I was even taller than some of my teachers! I could barely fit in any of the desks in any classroom, so my knees were constantly banging into the bottom of my desk. And since I'd shot up a few inches in just a few months, I felt like I was in some alien body. My legs and arms just wanted to do things all on their own.

There was only one good thing about constantly growing. It meant I had to keep buying new basketball shoes—and while I didn't care much about fashion, I was *totally* obsessed with basketball shoes. My newest pair had a herringbone pattern on the outsole for extra traction, a padded heel, and a lime green stripe and laces, which perfectly matched my green and yellow basketball uniform.

I was lacing up my new shoes in the locker room on the first day of basketball practice when my best friend, Avery, noticed them.

"Nice kicks," she said with a nod. "They're new, right?"

"Yeah, I outgrew my last pair in, like, three months," I replied. "Mom wasn't too thrilled to have to buy a new pair so soon, but what could she do? I mean, it's not my fault that I have enormous clown feet."

Avery laughed. "You do *not* have clown feet. They're in proportion to your body."

"Well, they *feel* like clown feet," I said, jumping up. "I keep tripping over them. Over my *own* feet. Have you ever done that?"

"No," Avery said. "But once I tied my shoelaces together by accident and I fell flat on my face."

I giggled. "No way!"

"Way," Avery replied. "It was not fun."

We both moved to the mirror, where I pulled my long blond hair back into a ponytail. Avery's hair was normally curly, but for basketball season she wore it in tight braids that went along the side of her head and hung down her back. The summer had turned me into a tall, gangly, pale beanpole (Mom's a sunscreen freak), but Avery had come back to school looking gorgeous, with contacts in her big brown eyes and a glowing tone to her brown skin. We looked so different that you might not believe we were best friends, but we had been since first grade, when we bonded over a mutual love of pizza and the Powerpuff Girls.

"Elle, you're frowning," Avery said, noticing my expression in the mirror. "Everything okay?"

"Yeah, I'm just a little nervous, I guess," I replied.

"What's there to be nervous about?" she asked. She looked around the locker room, where the other girls on the team were getting ready. "This is Spring Meadow. Everybody's going to make the team."

"I know," I said. "I'm just off my game right now."

"Are you kidding?" Avery said. "You're one of the best players we've got. There's nothing to worry about."

"I guess," I said, letting out an anxious breath.

We headed out to the school gym. Spring Meadow School was a small private school in Wilmington, Delaware. It was a K–12 school with only about fifty kids in each grade. So it was pretty amazing that we had ten girls interested in being on the basketball team.

I had been playing with most of the girls since fifth grade. Hannah Chambal and Natalie Saunders were best friends, and they were also both really nice. Caroline Lindgren was nice too, but she was one of our weaker players and spent most of her time on the bench. Bianca Hidalgo, Tiff Kalifeh, and Dina Garcia were all pretty tight with one another, and they were all good players. Patrice Ramirez was the daughter of our coach.

The only girl I hadn't played with yet was Amanda O'Connor. I'd heard that Coach Ramirez had convinced her to join the team this year, after Molly Porter moved away. Amanda was on the shorter side, and I didn't think she was sporty. She came to Spring Meadow a year ago, and she joined the choir and I think the school band, too. So I was a little curious to see what kind of an athlete she was.

We all started stretching to warm up, dressed in our practice uniforms: green shorts with a yellow stripe down the side, and green T-shirts with "Nighthawks" in yellow letters across the front, and a yellow bird on the back.

Coach Ramirez came out of her office and strolled onto the gym. She coached the middle school teams for Spring Meadow. For fifth and sixth grade, we'd been coached by Coach Friedman, a sixth-grade math teacher. He was so quiet that his nickname was "Coach Mouse." So I wondered what Coach Ramirez was like.

The first thing I learned was that she was not quiet at all.

"Good afternoon, Nighthawks!" Coach Ramirez said loudly. "Line up for me, please, two rows, five and five!"

We scrambled onto the gym floor. She had that kind of voice that made you hustle when she told you to do something. I ended up in the last row with Avery on my right and Amanda on my left.

"Give me ten squats!" Coach Ramirez ordered.

I dropped and started the warm-up. It felt good to be moving, and I could feel my nerves dropping away. We followed the squats with some old-school push-ups, sit-ups, and jumping jacks.

I glanced over at Amanda to see how she was doing. She had her reddish-brown hair pulled back in a messy ponytail, and her freckled cheeks were turning pink, but she was keeping up with everyone else.

"Nice job!" Coach called out when we finished our last jumping jack. "Welcome to the first day of practice. Today we're going to do some drills so I can figure out what positions you'll all be playing this year."

Bianca raised her hand. "Why can't we play the same positions we played last year?" she asked.

"Because Coach Friedman chose those positions, not me," Coach Ramirez replied. "I've seen most of you play, and I know what you can do, but a lot can change over the summer. Just look at Elle. She must have grown a foot since last year. She's going to be a monster on the court."

I could feel my own cheeks getting pink. Now everyone was expecting me to be great—just because I had suddenly become supersized. A "monster," Coach had called me. Nice.

Coach Ramirez pointed to the end of the court nearest her. A bunch of orange cones had been lined up on the end line, behind the basket.

"This drill is called twenty-one cones," she said. "Stay with the lines you're in now, and line up on the other end of the court."

Following her instructions, we formed two lines, one on each side of the free throw line. Avery, me, Amanda, Caroline, and Patrice stood on the left side. Tiff, Bianca, Dina, Hannah, and Natalie lined up on the right. Coach Ramirez tossed a basketball to Avery and one to Tiff.

"Here's how this one works. Shoot from the free throw line. If you make the shot, run to the other end of the court and grab a cone. Then bring it with you back to the line. The team that gets the most cones wins," she explained. "Got it?"

"Yes, Coach!" we all replied.

I stretched my arms, ready for action. Now that competition was in the mix, I was more eager than ever to do a good job.

Coach Ramirez put the whistle to her mouth.

Tweeeeeet!

Avery and Tiff shot for the basket at the same time. Avery's bounced off the rim. Tiff's swished through the net. She ran to grab a cone, grinning confidently. But then again, Tiff was always super confident. She worked out all the time, got straight As, and she even designed and sewed her own hijabs. She wore a green and yellow one to match the Nighthawks uniform at every game and practice.

It was my turn to shoot next, along with Bianca.

Swish! Swish! We both made our shots. I ran across the court to grab a cone—and ended up knocking over *two* cones when I picked up mine.

"Deluca, fix those!" Coach called out to me. I did it and quickly ran back to the line. Amanda had made her basket and ran past me, smiling.

Caroline shot next for our team, and she missed. So did Patrice.

"Line up the ball with your shooting eye next time, Ramirez!" Coach yelled at her daughter. Patrice bit her lip and moved to the back of the line.

I looked over at the other team. They had grabbed five cones already, and we only had a measly two. But then we quickly caught up. Avery made her shot, and I sank the ball on my next turn. I didn't knock over any cones this time, either.

Nope. Instead, I stumbled on my run back and had to stop myself from falling on my face. I looked to see if Coach Ramirez was watching. Of course she was, but she didn't say anything about it, thankfully.

The drill moved pretty quickly. Soon we had eight cones to the other team's ten. Patrice didn't miss a basket after that first one, and even Caroline managed to get one in. I only missed one.

My last shot bounced off the backboard and through the hoop. I ran back to get a cone—except there were none left. Instead, Bianca ran past me, triumphantly holding up the last cone.

"We win!" she cheered, and she and the other girls on her team started jumping up and down.

"Nice work, everybody," Coach Ramirez said. "Now we're going to all work on defense. But first, let's get these cones out of the way."

We quickly stacked the cones on the sidelines and then Coach explained the next drill to us. Two players would be on the court at a time—one playing offense, the other playing defense. The offensive player would have a few feet head start. On the whistle, the offensive player would dribble down the court and try to do a layup while the defensive player tried to block the shot.

"I don't want to see any fouls, am I clear?" she asked. "Everyone will have a turn in both positions. Bianca and Tiff, you're up first."

Coach blew the whistle, and they both sprinted down the court. Tiff's pretty fast, so she caught up to Bianca and got in front of her and tried to block the shot, but Bianca jumped up and got the layup pretty easily.

Caroline and Amanda went next, with Amanda on defense. Amanda was fast too, but I could tell that she was a little unsure of what to do once she caught up with Caroline. Caroline missed the shot, but not because of Amanda's pressure—she just came in at a bad angle.

Then it was my turn to block Avery. I caught up to her and when I pivoted to move in front of her, I accidentally bumped into her.

"No FOULS, Deluca!" Coach Ramirez yelled.

"Sorry, Coach!" I said, as Avery's layup swished through the net. I figured there was no point in making excuses to Coach Ramirez. What would I have said, anyway? *Uh, it was an accident because I still haven't gotten used to how my body works yet.* No way.

I did better when it came my turn to shoot. Coach had Dina guarding me, which was crazy, because while Dina's a good player she's one of the shortest on the team. I made an easy layup—and I didn't even trip!

After everybody had a turn shooting and defending, we did the drill from the other side of the court. That meant we had to dribble and finish with our left hand. I'm pretty comfortable on both sides of the court, so I nailed that shot too—even though Bianca jumped like a kangaroo to try to block me.

We did a few more drills after that one, and I was pretty sure I had done okay—not my best, but okay. Coach instructed us to cool down and disappeared into her office.

Avery and I sat on the bleachers.

"How'd I do?" Avery asked me. "I really want to play point guard again this year."

"You did great," I assured her. "And anyway, Coach *has* to make you a point guard. You're one of the best ball handlers we've got. You've got great control."

Avery smiled. "Thanks!"

"I'm not so sure about me, though," I said. "I

loved being a shooting guard last year. I got to take so many shots."

Avery nodded. "You did fine. Don't worry about it."

Coach Ramirez strolled back out, holding her clipboard.

"We're off to a good start," she said. "Not *great*, but good. I can tell that *some* of you made the extra effort to train over the summer. But others need to get back up to speed."

I saw Caroline look down at her feet, and I felt bad for her—we all knew Coach was talking about Caroline. Then it occurred to me that she might have been talking about me, too, and my palms started to sweat.

"To start the season, we'll work with you in the following positions," she said, looking down at her clipboard. "Deluca, you're center."

I almost fell off the bleachers. I knew I shouldn't interrupt Coach, but I couldn't stop myself.

"*Me?*" I asked. My mind was reeling. Center was maybe the toughest position to play. Besides being expected to stay open for passes, a center had to do a lot of blocking near the net, and be ready to pick up rebounds.

Coach nodded. "Yes, you. Hidalgo, you're—"

Bianca didn't even let her finish. "Coach, why aren't I playing center?" she asked, her dark eyes flashing. "I had a great record last year."

The rest of us got really quiet. We hadn't been working with Coach Ramirez that long, but we already knew that she wasn't the kind of coach you could challenge. This was a pretty bold move on Bianca's part.

Coach Ramirez lowered her clipboard and looked directly at Bianca.

"You're a great shot, Bianca," she said. "Which is why I'm making you our starting shooting guard. I've got to put Elle at center. She's taller than anybody on the court, and I'll guarantee you she's taller than any of the opponents we'll be playing. Her height gives us a huge advantage, and we need to use it wisely. And how we use it is *my* decision. Got that?"

"Yes, Coach," Bianca replied, but boy, did she look upset.

I guess I looked upset too, after hearing Coach's explanation. Did she make me center because I was the best shot, or the best at offense? No.

She gave me the position just because I was tall.

That meant I didn't get to be shooting guard. And Bianca was unhappy, and that wasn't cool, because Bianca loved drama. I am the opposite. I usually go out of my way to avoid it.

I sighed. My height was ruining my life again!

My Nightmare

C oach Ramirez read off the rest of the positions: Avery, Natalie, and Amanda would share duties as point guard. Tiff and Caroline would play power forward (although I guessed that Tiff would be doing most of the playing). Dina and Patrice were our small forwards. Hannah would play shooting guard along with Bianca, and Bianca would back me up as center.

After Bianca's interruption, nobody else dared say anything while Coach made the announcements.

"I'll see you all after school on Wednesday," she

said. "Practices are every Monday, Wednesday, and Friday, and our first game is this Sunday."

We all headed into the locker room to grab our backpacks and duffel bags. Since most of us got picked up right after practice, we showered and changed at home.

The gym is in the main building of the school, which is where the high school kids have classes. It also contains the cafeteria. The elementary school students and the middle schoolers (like me) each had our own building. But all the cool stuff was in the main building. The elementary kids had their own gym, but it was a lot smaller than the high school one.

Avery and I walked together to the vestibule by the school's main entrance to wait for our parents to arrive. It was school policy that everyone had to be picked up at the front entrance.

"I can't believe she made me center," I said to Avery in a low voice as we walked.

"Elle, that's so cool!" she said. "You'll be a great center."

I frowned. "I'm not so sure. And I really liked being a shooting guard."

We stopped in front of the main bulletin board, which featured a big poster.

Put on your dancing shoes!
It's time for the annual
SPRING MEADOW
FALL COTILLION
This Saturday!
First dancers begin at 5 p.m.

I looked at the poster and groaned. "Is that *this* Saturday?"

"Yeah. Don't you remember Mr. Patel saying that we start practicing in gym class tomorrow?" Avery asked.

"No," I admitted. "I was too busy pulling down my gym shorts the whole class, because they're way too short."

The annual fall cotillion is one of the weird things about our school—and not weird in a good way.

A cotillion is a fancy, formal kind of dance where everyone gets dressed up and boys and girls do old-fashioned dances together. It's been a tradition at the school for, like, a hundred years or something.

I know that other schools have fall dances too. At those, you can wear whatever you want. They play popular music and you don't have to dance if you don't want to. You don't even have to go!

But in my school, starting in seventh grade, everyone *has* to go to the cotillion. You even get a grade for it! My brother, Jim, says that almost everyone gets an A, and the grade is mostly to force you to show up.

I have been to cotillions to watch the dancing, because Jim has been dancing in them for the last five years. The seventh graders start first, and then each grade dances, up to the seniors. Then they serve punch and tiny sandwiches with the crusts cut off.

I never minded going as a kid, because it was kind of fun to watch the other kids dance. But last year it hit me that I would be up there dancing soon.

I'd have to wear a dumb, frilly dress and shoes that hurt and itchy tights and dance with some boy. I'd actually had a few nightmares about it.

And now it was only five days away.

"Wow, Elle, this cotillion isn't going to be easy for you, is it?"

I heard Bianca behind me and spun around.

"What do you mean?" I asked.

She smiled innocently. "Well, with you being so tall now, any boy you dance with will be so much shorter than you."

I hadn't even thought of that. I knew my face must have turned pale.

Bianca laughed. "Oh, well. Guess we'll see on Saturday!"

Then she waved. "My mom's here. See you tomorrow."

"Well, that was pretty mean of her," Avery remarked.

I groaned. "Maybe, but she's right! I'm going to be towering over any boy who dances with me. It's going to be awful!"

"It won't be so bad," Avery assured me. "The dance part only lasts, like, five minutes."

Then she looked at her phone. "Dad's outside. I'll see you tomorrow!"

Avery ran out, and I was left in the hallway with just a few other kids. One of them was Amanda, who approached me kind of shyly.

"Hi, Elle," she said. "That was, um, a fun practice today."

"So you liked it?" I asked her.

Amanda nodded. "Sure," she said. "I mean, I've always wanted to play on the team. I watch the WNBA all the time. I just didn't think I'd be good enough, but then Coach Ramirez asked me to play, and . . ."

"I thought you did great," I told her.

She smiled. "Thanks."

"I watch the WNBA all the time too," I told her. "Who's your favorite player?"

Amanda looked thoughtful. "Maybe Sue Bird of the Storm. I don't know, there's so many."

I nodded. "Yeah, she's great. Probably my all-time favorite is Sheryl Swoopes."

Amanda's green eyes flickered with recognition. "Oh yeah, she's, like, a legend, right?"

Before I got an answer, I felt my phone vibrate. **Outside.**

"My mom's here," I told her. "See you tomorrow!"

I walked to the car, thinking about how that was probably the longest conversation I'd ever had with Amanda, even though we'd gone to the same small school for a year. I had no idea that she was a WNBA fan, like I was, and I was glad she had joined the team. Besides, she had a really nice smile.

I climbed into the passenger seat next to Mom.

"Sorry I'm a little late, Elle," she said. "Crazy day. Now that Jim has his own car, I'm going to see if he can pick you up sometimes."

"That's cool," I said, strapping on my seat belt.

My Mom was one of the busiest people I knew. Besides taking care of me and Jim, she was home full time with my sister, Beth, who has special needs. Mom was also in the PTA and volunteered for every school event.

"So how was practice?" Mom asked.

"Well . . . ," I replied.

Mom looked surprised. "Not good?"

"Not *great*," I admitted. "My game's just not the same as it was. I keep tripping over my own feet and bumping into other players."

"You'll get more comfortable the more you practice," she assured me. She glanced down at my sneakers. "How'd the shoes fit?"

"Fine," I said. "But that reminds me: I need new gym shorts, like, right away. Mine don't fit anymore. They kept creeping up my butt and I had to keep pulling them down."

Mom frowned. "Well *that's* not good," she said. "We'll get you a pair at the school store tomorrow, before school starts. We'll just leave a little early."

"Thanks," I said. "We're starting dumb dance practice in gym tomorrow, and—"

"Oh my gosh!" Mom cried. "The cotillion is this Saturday, isn't it? I keep forgetting that we need to get you a dress."

Actually, Mom hadn't been forgetting. She'd

asked me a few times over the summer if we could go dress shopping, and each time I'd made up an excuse why I couldn't go.

"Well, maybe I don't *have* to wear a dress," I said, and then I had a sudden inspiration. "I could wear one of Jim's old suits! That's formal wear, right?"

"Don't be silly, Elle, of course you have to wear a dress," Mom replied. "It's one of the rules of the cotillion. Appearance is part of your grade."

"*Appearance?* Seriously? Well that's pretty ridiculous, don't you think?" I asked.

Mom sighed. "I . . . you're probably right, but it's a school tradition, and traditions are important," she said. "You have no practice on Thursday, so we can go to the mall. It will be fun! We can get you a nice dress for the cotillion, and maybe even some other things you need. We can spruce up your wardrobe! We haven't had a clothes shopping trip in ages."

Again, the reason for that was not Mom's fault—whenever she'd asked, I'd found some excuse not to go.

"Do we have to go?" I asked, even though I knew the answer.

"Yes," Mom replied, and she shook her head. "Honestly, what twelve-year-old girl doesn't want to go on a shopping spree?"

This *twelve-year-old girl*, I thought, but I didn't say it out loud. I knew that Mom was just being nice, and she honestly thought I would have fun shopping with her. I didn't know how to explain to her how rotten it felt to get dressed up in fancy clothes, and to have to dance with a boy.

I stared out the window for the rest of the drive home, wallowing in my misery.

I didn't get to be a shooting guard anymore. I'd have to spend every day in gym learning to dance with some boy. And Thursday night, I'd have to go try on girly clothes at the mall.

This week was going to be the worst!

The Giraffe and the Monkey

The next morning, Mom dropped me off at school early so I could buy new gym shorts from the school store. I didn't mind waking up a few minutes early, because on most days my routine was the same: I put my hair in a ponytail, threw on a T-shirt and jeans, wolfed down breakfast, brushed my teeth, and headed out the door.

Even though Spring Meadow was a private school, they didn't make us wear uniforms, and I was happy about that. If I had to walk around in a short, plaid skirt, and button-down blouse all day, I'd have been miserable. But we did have to wear uniform shorts and T-shirts for gym glass. The school had a little shop in a room next to the main office that sold the gym clothes, plus other spirit wear and Spring Meadow banners, tote bags, water bottles, and stuff like that.

I went inside and found Mrs. Wilson there. She was very tiny and had white hair and some kids joked that she'd been with the school since it began in the early twentieth century. Which was kind of mean, but I guess it was true that she looked very old.

"Good morning, Elle!" she said, smiling at me. Old or not, she knew every single kid in the school by name, which was impressive. "How can I help you this morning?"

"I need new gym shorts, please," I said, and I told her my size.

"Looks like you had a growth spurt over the summer," she said. "My, you got tall!"

"Yes, ma'am," I answered politely. Usually it was annoying when people said that because it's like, do they think I don't know that? *Oh really, I'm tall? I didn't realize. Thanks for letting me know.* But Mrs. Wilson was so sweet that it didn't bother me.

I paid for the shorts, stuffed them in my gym bag, and headed over to the middle school building to homeroom. Avery was already there, and I slid into the seat next to her. As usual, Avery was dressed in a cute skirt and shirt. She always looked like she was ready to go to a café in France or something while I . . . well, I pretty much always looked like I just rolled out of bed.

Before I could even say hi, the bell rang and the speaker in the classroom began to crackle.

"Good morning, Spring Meadow students and staff!" The cheerful voice of Principal Lubin came over the sound system. "Friday we'll be having a pep rally eighth period to kick off basketball season, so get a good sleep the night before and be sure to eat your veggies! Don't come to school too pooped to pep!"

Some kids groaned. Principal Lubin was the corniest human on the planet and loved to make silly jokes all the time.

"Then Saturday night, our students in grades seven through twelve will be putting on their finest duds for our annual cotillion! Everyone is invited to come watch," he said.

A bunch of kids cheered that, but it was my turn to groan. The thought of *everyone* watching me dance didn't exactly make me happy.

"Have a great day everybody, and remember: Be kind to one another! Now, let's all stand for the Pledge of Allegiance."

We obeyed, and then our homeroom teacher, Ms. Ebear, spoke up.

"All right, settle down everybody so I can take attendance," she said. "I know the dance is very exciting, but you'll have plenty of time to talk about it at lunch."

I was so lucky to get Ms. Ebear for homeroom, because she was my favorite teacher. She was really smart and interesting, and she when she taught history, she made it about stories and people and not just boring names and dates. She wore her shiny brown hair in a neat bob, and she wore these severe black eyeglasses that Avery called "hipster" glasses, but I think they made her look totally cool.

When the next bell rang, I stayed right where I was, because I had World History first period with Ms. Ebear in the same classroom. I waved good-bye to Avery.

"See you in gym!" she called out, and remembering that today we were going to be dancing, I groaned again.

Hannah walked into class and sat down next to me, followed by Natalie, who sat right behind her.

"What's the matter, Elle? I thought you liked gym?"

"I like gym," I replied. "But I don't like dancing."

"No? I'm looking forward to it," Hannah said. "My parents would never let me go to a dance unless it was required by the school."

"And they're okay with you being paired up with some rando guy?" Natalie asked, cleaning her eyeglasses on the edge of her T-shirt as she spoke. "My mom thinks it's kind of weird."

"Well, you know, back in India arranged marriages

are very common," Hannah pointed out. "So they don't think it's weird. Anyway, it kind of takes the pressure off, doesn't it? You don't have to worry if some guy will ask you to the dance or not. Nobody gets left out that way."

"I guess," I said. "But what if you don't want to dance at all?"

"Then I guess you're stuck," Natalie replied. "Well, I'm psyched because I got a new dress! It matches the pink in my hair."

She twirled a streak of her dark-blond hair, which she'd dyed bright pink before school started.

Before I could complain again about wearing a dress, the bell rang. Ms. Ebear sat on the edge of her desk.

"All right, where did we leave off yesterday?" she asked.

Several hands shot up.

"Dylan," she said.

"We were talking about how the caravan trade across the Sahara changed life in Western Africa," Dylan replied.

"Right!" Ms. Ebear said. "Now think about this: If you're traveling across the desert to trade, you're going to bring more than just your camel with you. You're going to bring your language, your traditions, your religion, and even your laws."

That was how Ms. Ebear taught—by making you feel like you were experiencing history yourself, not just reading about it. By the end of class, I swear I felt much hotter than I did at the start of class, as if we'd just been traveling across the Sahara Desert.

My next class was Earth Science with Ms. Rashad. Because we were studying medieval Africa in World History, Ms. Rashad was teaching us about African ecosystems. When I walked into the classroom, she was projecting a diagram of an African savanna on the screen.

In science class, I got to sit next to my other best friend, Blake Tanaka. He lived next door, so we'd known each other since I can remember. Our moms often took turns driving us to school.

"Did you get your practice schedule yet?" he

asked. "I finally saved up allowance for the new NBA 2K game. We have got to play it. It looks awesome."

"Monday, Wednesday, Friday, right after school," I told him.

Blake nodded. "Yeah, we practice on the same nights, but at five. So no practice today! You should come over."

"Sure, maybe," I said.

Bianca and Tiff came in and walked past us.

"Hi, Blake," Bianca said, flashing him her model-worthy smile. Then she and Tiff began giggling as they walked off.

I looked at Blake and saw that he was blushing. "No way! Do you like her?" I whispered.

"No! I mean—I don't know, I guess I'm just not used to girls, you know, noticing me," he said.

Blake had always been a chubby kid, even though he'd been playing basketball for years, just like me. Then he'd had a growth spurt over the summer, and he came back looking pretty toned. Avery called him a "certified hottie." Which I guess he is, but to me he's just Blake and he always will be.

I rolled my eyes at him. "Oh, boy. Don't let it go to your head!"

"Hey, can't you just let me enjoy the feeling?" Blake asked like he was mad, but he was smiling at me.

Then the bell rang and we quieted down. Ms. Rashad wasn't as interesting as Ms. Ebear, but the subject matter was pretty cool. We watched a film about animals of the African savanna. Cheetahs raced across the grassy fields, lions chased zebras, monkeys groomed one another, and impossibly tall giraffes munched on leaves from the treetops.

I stared at the giraffes, the tallest animals on the savanna, even taller than the elephants. I imagined what a scientist would think coming into this classroom and seeing me, towering over everybody else, looking ridiculous sitting at my tiny desk.

I was the giraffe of Spring Meadow School, I thought. Oh, well. At least giraffes were cute.

My next class was the one I'd been dreading: gym. I met up with Avery in the locker room. We quickly changed and headed out to the gym, where our teacher, Mr. Patel, was waiting for us.

All of the kids knew what was up, and the girls and the boys separated and awkwardly stood around, waiting for the dancing to start.

"Okay, everybody, don't be nervous," Mr. Patel began. "Dancing is fun, it's easy, and it's athletic. We're going to start off learning a few simple steps. But first, everybody needs a partner. Boys, line up over there and face me."

The boys obeyed. Some of them were grumbling, and a few were nervously looking down at their feet. I grinned at Blake and he made a face at me.

Mr. Patel faced the girls. "Okay, Hannah, you're with Jacob. Natalie, you're with Ethan. Amanda, you're with Alex. Avery, you're with Matthew."

As Mr. Patel named the pairings, I crossed my fingers behind my back, hoping I would get Blake. Having him as my partner would at least make this nightmare bearable, I thought.

But then I saw Bianca go up to Mr. Patel and say something. She flashed him her model-worthy smile.

"All right, Bianca," he said. "You're with Blake."

I felt my hopes wash away as Bianca walked up to Blake. Then she turned to me and smirked—almost as if she'd known that I wanted him to be my partner. But that wouldn't have been too hard to figure out. Everyone knew Blake and I were good friends.

I was so bummed that I tuned out Mr. Patel, and then I heard him repeating my name.

"Elle! Ms. Deluca! You're with Dylan," he said.

I looked down the line of boys at Dylan, who was nervously fidgeting in place, and my heart sank.

Dylan was the shortest boy in the class.

I didn't protest—I didn't want to hurt Dylan's feelings—so I walked over to Dylan.

"Hey, Elle!" he said, smiling. "So, um, we're partners. Cool!"

Besides being the shortest boy in the class, Dylan was always in motion. If there was a chair in his way, he'd jump over it. If there was a bar to hang from, he'd hang from it. He reminded me of one of the monkeys from the savanna video, and then an image of a giraffe and a monkey dancing together popped into my head, and I couldn't get it out.

Then Mrs. Wilson came into the gym.

"My lovely dance partner is here!" Mr. Patel said. "Are you ready, Mrs. Wilson?"

"I'm always ready for dancing!" she replied.

Mr. Patel looked at us. "Okay, everyone, we're going to start with a basic box step. For now, everyone turn and face me."

We did, and Mr. Patel started to show us how to do the step. "Okay, this is called a box step because you will be taking steps in the shape of a square," Mr. Patel explained. "First, put your weight on your right foot and step forward with your left, like this. Then step to the side on the right foot and bring your feet together."

He and Mrs. Wilson demonstrated as he talked.

"Now, let me see you do that," Mr. Patel said, when they'd finished.

We repeated his movements, and I did it without tripping over my feet.

So far, so good, I thought.

"Now step back with your right foot, step to the side with your left foot, and bring your feet together again," Mr. Patel instructed. "Do it with me. See? We just made a box."

I was too nervous to even glance over at Dylan to see how he was doing. Up ahead, I saw Bianca whisper something to Blake, and he laughed.

"All right, let's put it all together," Mr. Patel said. "Let's say the movements out loud as we go. Forward, side, together. Back, side, together."

"Forward, side, together," I mumbled, as I did the steps. "Back, side, together."

We repeated them a few times, and I was actually starting to feel confident. I was getting the hang of it!

Then all of the rules changed.

"Great job!" Mr. Patel encouraged us. "Okay, now everyone face your partner."

I turned and looked at Dylan, who had an awkward, shy grin on his face.

Mr. Patel raised his left hand. "Boys, take your partner by the hand," he said, and he held Mrs. Wilson's right hand.

Dylan grabbed my right hand.

"Now, put your free hands on each other's shoulders," Mr. Patel instructed.

That's when things got really awkward. Dylan had to stretch up to reach my shoulder, and I had to crouch down to put my hand on his.

"Here's where it gets tricky," Mr. Patel said. "Boys, you will do the box step like we learned, starting with your left foot. But girls, you must start on your *right* foot."

Wait, what? I thought. We had just learned the dance one way, and now I had to do the opposite—just because I was a girl. Before I could process this, Mr. Patel was off and running.

"And, begin! Forward, side, together. Back, side, together!"

I was so mixed up! I started off on my left foot again, and Dylan and I went in different directions.

"Sorry!" I apologized.

"That's okay," Dylan said sweetly. We stopped and waited for the pattern to start again.

"Forward, side, together!"

This time I started off on my right foot, but when

it came time to move backward, I stepped with my right foot again. I shook my head.

"This is confusing," I muttered.

"Let's try again," Dylan said. "Forward, side, together."

I stepped off on my right foot . . . and landed right on Dylan's foot! He started to stumble and I had to grab him.

"Sorry!" I groaned again.

"It's okay," Dylan said.

I could feel my face turning bright red. I was positive that everyone was staring at me. I glanced to the right and saw Bianca and Blake doing the steps perfectly.

I felt so bad for Dylan. He was being so nice about everything. He deserved a better partner than me.

I couldn't wait for gym to be over!

One-on-One

"Forward, side, together. Back, side, together."
Natalie was still muttering the box step
directions to herself at lunchtime that day.

I groaned. "Please don't remind me of gym class
right now."

Lunchtime is one of my favorite times to chill
during the day. The cafeteria had big glass win-
dows that looked out over a grassy meadow—the
same meadow the school was named after. The
food wasn't fancy, but it was always healthy, and
there was an awesome salad bar. I ate at a table

with my closest friends from the basketball team: Avery (of course), Hannah, Natalie, Caroline, and Patrice.

I was eating an enormous salad with grilled chicken, tomatoes, cucumbers, and chickpeas, but Natalie was taking me out of my happy place.

"Sorry, Elle, I just don't want to forget the steps," Natalie said.

"It wasn't so bad, was it?" Avery asked me.

"Are you kidding?" I asked. "It was awful! I couldn't get any of the steps right."

"Well, we have all week to learn," Hannah piped up helpfully.

"Oh, good. All week," I said in a flat voice.

Avery nudged me. "Maybe the problem is that you're approaching it with a negative attitude," she said. "Come on, try to think of something positive about gym class today."

Avery's mom was a yoga instructor, so Avery was always talking about negative and positive energy and the flow of her chi and stuff like that, so I was used to it.

"All right," I said. "I didn't fall on my face. That's positive, right?"

Avery giggled. "Yes. Come on. One more."

"Well . . . I didn't have to keep pulling down my gym shorts," I replied.

"Awesome!" Avery said. "See, doesn't that make you feel better?"

I shook my head. "Not really."

"I've got one," Patrice said, leaning across the table. "Your dance partner, Dylan, is cute."

I couldn't help myself—I made a face. "Uh, I guess."

"Ooh, do you like him?" Caroline asked Patrice.

"No! He's just cute," Patrice said quickly.

"Maybe, but he is not the *cutest* boy in gym class," Hannah said. "That's Alex."

I dug into my salad and tried to tune everyone out. I noticed that over the summer, some of my friends had started to get totally boy crazy! Thankfully, Avery wasn't one of them.

"I need a dose of positive energy right now," I whispered to Avery.

She handed me a chocolate chip cookie. "Here you go," she said with a grin.

I took the cookie from her. Avery was right. I had to stop being so negative. But when I tried to think of something else positive about the cotillion—well, I just couldn't.

After school, Blake's mom picked up me and Blake.

"How are you today, Elle?" Mrs. Tanaka asked me.

"Good, thanks," I replied. I wasn't going to bother her with my whole dance story.

"Mom, can Elle come over and play NBA LIVE 18 with me?" Blake asked.

"You know the rule, Blake," his mom replied. "No video games on weekdays. I want you to concentrate on your homework, especially now that practice has started."

"But I only have, like, one worksheet," Blake argued.

"The rule is the rule," she said. "Besides, it is a beautiful day out."

"So can I practice basketball at Elle's first, then?" Blake asked.

Mrs. Tanaka nodded. "Yes. The exercise will do you good."

Blake turned around to look at me. "You ready to lose at one-on-one?"

I grinned. "I should be asking *you* that question."

Blake and I lived on the same street in Greenmont, a small town in Delaware that's near the small city of Wilmington. The drive home took us past Main Street, which had a movie theater, restaurants, and some small shops. Next came the town park, which had a small dog park attached to it. Then a few blocks down was our street, Carrie Lane.

Mrs. Tanaka pulled up in front of my house, and Blake and I jumped out.

"Thanks, Mrs. T," I said.

"You're welcome, Elle," she replied. "You two have fun."

Blake's mom had been right—it was a beautiful day, still warm even though it was fall. We dumped our backpacks on the front lawn and I ran and grabbed a basketball from the box of sports equipment we keep next to the garage. I started dribbling with my back to the free-standing basketball net on the end of my driveway.

"Come and get me," I taunted Blake, spinning and taking off toward the hoop.

"Who said *you* get the ball first? No fair!" Blake protested.

"My house," I replied, and then I drove up for a layup that bounced off the backboard and swished through the net.

I caught the ball as it came back. "One–nothing," I said, tossing the ball to Blake.

"What are we playing to?" he asked.

"How about twelve?" I answered, and he nodded.

He dribbled toward the hoop, faked right, then zagged left to get a clear shot of the basket. It bounced off the backboard, right back into his hands.

"Better luck next time," I teased, as he tossed the ball to me.

Mom came out the side door. "I thought I heard you guys. Hi, Blake," she said. "Elle, do you have homework?"

"A little," I replied, jumping up over Blake's head to sink another basket. "Can I do it after dinner?"

"Sure thing," Mom said, and then retreated inside.

Blake and I kept going with our game. Blake made his next shot, and the score kept slowly creeping up. Elle 4, Blake 2. Elle 6, Blake 3. Elle 8, Blake 6. By the time I made my twelfth basket, the score was 12–10.

Blake shook his head. "Lucky break. How about we play HORSE?"

HORSE is a shooting game where the players take turns shooting at the basket from anywhere they want on the court. After the first player shoots, the second player has to make the exact same shot from the exact same spot. If the second player misses, he or she gets a letter in the word "horse." Once a player spells out H-O-R-S-E, they're out and the other player wins.

"Sure," I said. "I'll even let you go first this time."

Blake stood about where the free throw line would be, centered in front of the hoop. He made a shot that swished through the net.

"Sa-woosh!" he said, laughing. "You've got to get it in without the backboard."

"No problem," I said. I positioned myself where Blake had stood, aimed carefully, and launched the shot.

The ball hit the edge of the rim and bounced back to me.

"Yes!" Blake cheered. "You get an *H*!"

"You got lucky," I told him. I moved to the left side of the driveway and positioned my shot. "This is more fun than practice, anyway."

"I thought you lived for practice?" Blake asked, as I made a basket.

"I used to," I said. "That was before I grew ten feet overnight and became a total klutz."

Blake took his shot, and made it. "Shut down!" he said. Then he dribbled toward the net for a layup. "And you're not a total klutz. You just wiped the court with me a few minutes ago."

"I guess," I said. "But it's just not the same."

"You know, you weren't a great player when you first started the game," Blake reminded me. "But you got great because you practiced and worked hard. So just keep doing that."

I nodded. "That makes sense," I agreed. "I could probably do that for the stupid dance, too. Maybe I could be good at it if I practiced. But I don't want to! It's such a waste of time!"

"I know what you mean," Blake said.

I was fired up now. "I don't want to dance with boys! I don't want to wear some dumb dress and be on display in front of everyone!"

"But you're on display when you play basketball," Blake said.

"It's not the same," I said. "Basketball is about skill and competition. And yeah, I know that dancers work hard and can be athletic and all that too. But that's not what the cotillion is about. It's not like they make everyone play basketball, right? So why does everyone have to dance?"

"Good point!" Blake agreed. "It's too bad we didn't get to be dance partners. Then we could just goof around and not stress about it."

We had been playing the whole time we talked. Blake had H-O-R, and I had H-O-R-S. One letter away from losing. It was Blake's turn. He moved to the front of the hoop. He stood with his back to the net.

"You're not serious," I said.

"Classic HORSE move," Blake told me. "It has to be tried at least once."

He tossed the ball back over his head—and he made the basket!

"All right," I said. "If you can do it, I can do it."

I stood with my back to the basket. I looked over my shoulder, then back. Then I threw the ball.

I turned around quickly to see it bounce off the backboard.

"H-O-R-S-E!" Blake cheered, pointing at me. "I win!"

"Lucky break," I said, and then I began dribbling the ball around the driveway. Over the summer

Jim had taught me a dribbling trick called a double crossover, and I'd been having fun with it ever since and trying to perfect it.

"What's that?" Blake asked.

"It's a double crossover," I told him. I planted my legs apart and bent at the knees. "You dribble with one hand, push over to the other hand, and push back to the beginning hand."

I demonstrated it standing still, and then put the move in motion. "It's good for confusing defenders, keeping them on their toes."

"Let me try!" Blake said, and I passed him the ball.

He started trying out the move.

"So, that was weird that Bianca asked to be your partner," I said. "She's a really good dancer, though, so I guess you're lucky."

Blake shrugged. "She's good. But I'd rather chill and have fun with you," he said.

"Thanks," I said. Then I stole the ball from him and made a basket.

"Hey, no fair!" he yelled, and I passed the ball to

him, laughing. "Come on, another game of one-on-
one. I need redemption."

"Sure," I said.

I was lucky to have a friend like Blake. For the
rest of the afternoon, I didn't even think about the
dance.

From Bad to Worse

The next day, Wednesday, I walked into gym class like a zombie. I actually even thought about pretending to be sick, but I knew if I did that I would have to miss practice. And even though I was still not happy about being center, I had decided to take Blake's advice and just work really hard at it. So missing practice was not an option.

"All right everyone, line up and face your partners," Mr. Patel announced at the start of class. Mrs. Wilson was there too, just like the day before.

"Oh, wait," Mr. Patel said. "Dylan and Alex, I want you two to switch partners. Alex and Elle are closer in height."

I could feel my face flush after being called out like that. Had Dylan asked to switch? More likely, Mr. Patel had noticed what a mess I'd been, dancing with Dylan yesterday.

Alex's partner had been Amanda, and Dylan looked pretty relieved as he walked over to her. As for Alex, well, I couldn't tell what he was thinking. He walked over to me and nodded. Alex had wavy, sandy-blond hair, and he was about five-foot-five, which made him one of the tallest boys in the class. So at least I wasn't looking over the top of his head.

"Yesterday most of you did a pretty good job with the box step," Mr. Patel began. "Today we're going to make it look nice, add a few extra moves, and add some music."

He took Mrs. Wilson by the hand and put his hand on her shoulder.

"Let's perfect our dance posture," he said. "Boys, you're what's known as the lead dancer. When you join hands with your partner, both of you should keep your elbows at shoulder height. And leads, your hand should be under your partner's shoulder blade."

Alex and I had to step closer to each other so he could put his hand on my back. It was super awkward.

"Girls, your left hand should be on your partner's shoulder," he said, and Mrs. Wilson demonstrated. "Now stand with your backs straight and your knees loose."

He paused, scanning the dancers. "No slouching, Jake!" he yelled. And then he yelled at *me*. "No slouching, Elle!"

Now, this was completely unfair. How was I supposed to keep my back straight while at the same time keeping my elbow at shoulder height? I had to crouch down to do that. So basically, what he was asking me to do was impossible!

I didn't argue. What was the point? So I straightened up.

"All right, now let's do the box step again a

few times," Mr. Patel instructed. "Forward, side, together. Back, side, together."

Alex was a better dancer than Dylan. He moved confidently and quickly, which didn't make things any easier for me. He was going so fast that I couldn't keep up.

"Elle, it's *this* way," he said when I moved left while he moved to my right.

"Sorry, it's so fast," I apologized.

"Good!" Mr. Patel called out. "Now, let's add some turns."

He started whirling around the gym with Mrs. Wilson. They turned their bodies as they did the box step, moving across the floor. They made it look easy, but when Alex tried to lead me in a turn, I got confused and stepped back with my left foot when I was supposed to step forward.

I looked around. Other kids were getting it right. Blake and Bianca were doing it perfectly—although Blake was moving much more slowly than Alex was.

Finally I gave up trying to do the box step and I just let Alex lead me around the gym floor, moving my feet in whatever direction he took me. Mr. Patel noticed.

"Elle, focus," he said. "Concentrate on the steps and let Alex lead you in the turns. Forward, side, together. Back, side, together."

I took a deep breath and looked down at my feet.

Forward, side, together. Back, side, together. . . .

Bam! I smacked right into someone. I looked up—and it was Bianca!

"Watch where you're going, Elle!" she snapped. "You nearly ran me over like a truck!"

My face got hot. How embarrassing!

"Sorry, Bianca," I mumbled.

Amanda and Dylan danced up to us. "Elle, you would be awesome in a mosh pit," Amanda said, smiling. Then she let go of Dylan's hands and bumped into him. "We should start one at the cotillion."

Blake let go of Bianca's hands. "Yeah!" he said, and then he bumped into Dylan, who grinned and bumped him back.

A couple of other kids started slamming into each other, mosh-pit style. Mr. Patel blew his whistle.

"Settle down, everybody!" Mr. Patel warned. "There will definitely not be a mosh pit at the cotillion. Now, get back to your positions."

I flashed Amanda a grateful smile and faced Alex again. I wish I could say that by the end of gym class we were dancing gracefully with each other, but we definitely were not. Mr. Patel kept asking us to add turns and fancy moves and they just made me more and more confused.

I had much higher hopes for practice that afternoon, but that didn't go so smoothly either. After we warmed up, Coach Ramirez had us do some drills, both offensive and defensive. First we lined up in two lines of five girls each, facing one another. I faced Avery.

"We're going to practice a defensive move called boxing out," Coach explained. "Patrice, come demonstrate with me."

Patrice ran and faced her mom.

"Okay, so Patrice is on offense," Coach said. "When she takes the shot, I'm going to box her out."

Coach held out her right arm and bent it at the elbow. She took a step toward Patrice, and then pivoted around so that her back was to Patrice.

"You put up your right hand, and turn to the left," she said, demonstrating again. "Then hold up both arms so you're ready for the rebound."

She nodded at Patrice, who moved back to her place in line. Then she pointed to Avery's line. "Okay, that's the offensive line. Defense, let me see you box out."

Why did it have to be another box? I wondered. But this move was easier for me than the box step, because I understood why I was doing it. I could picture using it on the court, after the player I was guarding took a shot.

"Right hand, turn, and box out!" Coach called out. I did the move with the rest of the players in line with me.

"Hands *up*, not behind you, when you finish," Coach yelled. "Elle, you need to pay attention. As center you need a strong defensive game."

I nodded and we repeated it again. Both Caroline and Dina forgot to put their hands up, but Coach didn't yell at them.

It was all because I was playing center, I knew it. It was a key position on the team, and Coach Ramirez was going to be hard on me. Which was super unfair, because I didn't even *want* to be center.

Still, I remembered what Blake had said, so I concentrated and kept at it. The next drill was a layup drill called the Mikan drill. You approach the basket and shoot first with your right hand, then take two steps to the left and shoot with your left hand. Then you take two steps to the right and shoot with your right hand again.

"When you shoot, I want to see you try to go off on one foot," Coach said. "When you make the right-handed layup, shoot off the left foot. And shoot off the right foot when you make a left-handed layup."

I had always liked making shots from the court better than doing layups; I think it's because you have to think more about what your feet are doing when you do a layup. So I knew this would be a good drill for me to practice.

I just wasn't expecting to be so bad at it.

"Shoot off your left foot, Elle!" Coach scolded me when I took my right-handed shot. "You're jumping off with both feet."

"Yes, Coach," I said, but when I moved to the left side of the hoop, I did the same thing.

We did the drill for a few minutes, and each of us had a few chances to do it. When we finished, Coach threw me the ball.

"Elle, go to the other hoop and do that ten more times," she told me.

I took the ball down the court and repeated the drill, while she led the other girls in a dribbling drill.

"Well, that was humiliating," I told Avery as we walked out of the locker room together after practice.

"What was humiliating?" she asked.

"Being singled out like that," I replied.

"Oh, that?" Avery asked. "Well, it's not like you were the only one. She had Caroline and Patrice practice passing, and she made Hannah and Natalie do extra shots from the foul line. I think she's just focusing on all our individual skills, you know?"

I hadn't realized any of that. "Oh, okay," I said. "I guess I'm just feeling self-conscious. I blame it on dance practice in gym."

Then Amanda walked up to us. "By the way, thanks for sticking up for me before," I told her.

She grinned. "No problem," she said, glancing at Bianca. "Anyway, I think you're a good dancer. You just have a bad partner."

I smiled back at her, and for the first time I noticed that she wore a blue and purple friendship bracelet around her wrist. *Who wore the matching one?* I wondered. I knew she had friends at school, but I didn't remember ever seeing her with a best friend.

Coach's whistle blew, interrupting my thoughts. "Practice game! Elle, Hannah, Avery, Caroline, Amanda on one team; Bianca, Tiff, Patrice, Dina, Natalie on the other. Bianca, you're center for your team."

We took our positions on the court. Bianca and I faced each other. I knew she was a much better dancer than I was. But standing there, face-to-face with her, it hit me: On the basketball court, my height was definitely an advantage. Bianca was tall, but she was still about six inches shorter than I was. And when you're playing center, height matters.

Coach threw the ball in. Bianca and I both jumped up, but my hand reached the ball first and I tapped it away. Hannah got it but Tiff quickly stole it from her. She passed it to Natalie, who took a shot at the basket.

The ball bounced hard and fast off the backboard, and I grabbed the rebound. Then I took off across the court, flying toward the basket while Bianca tried to catch up to me.

She didn't. I jumped for the layup and sank the ball in the basket.

"Nice breakaway layup!" Avery congratulated as she jogged past me.

I grinned. It felt good to finally get a win that day—even if it was just one basket.

A Ray of Hope . . .

The smell of Mom's slow cooker chili hit my nose as I entered the house after practice that day. I quickly showered and changed. I was setting the table for dinner when Mom came in pushing my sister, Beth, in her wheelchair.

Beth is four years older than I am. She was born deaf and blind, with cerebral palsy and autism. So all the things that I do with my eyes and ears, Beth does with touch, smell, and taste.

I walked over to Beth, leaned down, and hugged her. She sniffed the top of my head—that's how she knew it was me hugging her. She started shaking her head, so I knew she was happy to see me.

Then Beth grabbed my hand. She used her hand to form a symbol in my palm.

Eat.

I formed the same symbol back in her palm. *Eat.* When Beth was little, my mom and the specialists who worked with her tried to teach her sign language, but it was too complicated. So Mom and Beth's babysitter at the time came up with some simple symbols that worked. I was just a little kid when that was all happening, so I don't remember that time very well. But as soon as I learned to read in first grade, Mom taught me the signs, and I've been able to communicate with Beth ever since.

I sat down next to Beth and held her hand.

"Eddie! Jim! Dinner!" Mom called out.

Eddie is my dad. He came in first, kissed my mom, and then put the slow cooker on the table. My dad was six-foot-one, so I was still not taller than him yet.

"But that day will come soon," Dad always said. "You've still got a lot of growing to do, Elle."

My mom was five-nine, so I wasn't sure where I got my height from. Jim was pretty tall too—six-two—so we must both have inherited some random giant gene or something.

Even though I didn't inherit my height from my parents, I definitely looked like a cross between them. I had Mom's blond hair and Dad's hazel eyes. Beth had Dad's dark hair and hazel eyes like me. Jim had brown hair too, and he was the only one in the family with brown eyes. (Mom's were blue.)

Mom set down a salad and a plate of cornbread when my brother, Jim, came in. He was dressed in his football practice uniform, in everything but the pads. Two years ago, Jim switched from basketball to football, and he was so good at it that it looked like he might get to play college ball. He still played basketball for fun, though.

"Gotta eat and run," Jim said. He hugged Beth before he sat down.

Mom put some chili in Beth's bowl and started feeding her.

"This is the first time we're all at the table since Elle's big news," Mom said. "Tell everyone, Elle."

At first I didn't know what she was talking about, but then it hit me. "Oh, you mean that I'm starting center?"

"Elle, that's great!" my dad said. "You are really improving as a player."

"That's not why Coach Ramirez made me center," I pointed out. "It's because I'm freakishly tall."

"Elle, do not use that word to describe yourself," Mom scolded. "You are not freakish. You are exactly the way you are supposed to be."

"Okay, how about *unusually* tall then?" I asked.

"I remember when I went through my growth spurt a few years ago," Jim chimed in. "I'm still getting used to not having to reach so high for the hoop. Has it given you better hops?"

"It's hard to tell, because I keep tripping over my own feet at practice," I told him. "Did that happen to you?"

Jim laughed. "Yeah, of course it did!" he said. "Don't worry. You'll get more comfortable soon. You just need to keep practicing."

I nodded. "Yeah, that's what Blake said."

I spooned some chili into my bowl and put some salad on my plate. I suddenly realized I was ravenous after a day of dancing and basketball practice.

"So Elle, don't forget we're going to the mall tomorrow after school, to go shopping for the cotillion," Mom said.

I groaned. "How could I forget?"

Mom shook her head. "Honestly, Elle, I don't see what's so terrible about going shopping for new clothes."

"I'm just not *into* clothes, you know that," I replied. "I don't care about fashion. It's so confusing—there are too many choices. Skinny jeans and boyfriend jeans and crop tops and heels and wedges. I just want plain jeans and sweatshirts."

"Well, you can't wear that to the cotillion," Mom said. "Don't worry, I'll help you pick something out."

"Is Elle really dancing in the cotillion?" Dad

asked, frowning. "Already? Isn't she a little young to be dancing with boys and paraded around in front of everybody?"

"Exactly!" I cried, surprised and happy that Dad was taking my side. "I am definitely too young, and anyway, what does age have to do with it? Why should *anybody* be paraded around in a dress if they don't want to?"

Dad looked at my mom. "She has a point, Jeni," he said.

I had a flash of hope. Could my parents get me out of the cotillion?

"Elle does have a point," Mom conceded. "But participation in the cotillion is a requirement of the school. And going to a great school like Spring Meadow is worth the compromise. Besides, Elle, it is healthy to do things out of your comfort zone."

"Compromise," Mom had said. That wasn't a word I heard her use often. She bought everything Made in the USA, and wouldn't buy her makeup from companies that tested on animals.

I challenged her. "Mom, when have you ever compromised your beliefs?" I asked her.

Jim looked impressed. "And Elle swoops in with infallible logic!"

Mom frowned. "You've got me there, Elle," she said. "You've definitely given me something to think about."

"Does that mean we don't have to go dress shopping tomorrow?" I asked hopefully.

"No, it does not," Mom said. "We are still going."

I leaned back in my chair and groaned—and then I had an idea. "Can we ask Avery to come with us, at least?"

I knew that Avery already had her dress, but she loved going to the mall. Having her there would make it more fun—and she might be able to help me pick out a dress that didn't make me look like a fancy dork.

"Of course," Mom said. "Go ahead and ask her."

Dad turned to Jim. "And how is football practice going?" he asked.

"Pretty good," Jim replied. "Coach wants to try me out as a tight end, so I've got to work on my blocking game."

Most Deluca family dinner conversation was about sports. Both of my parents played sports in high school—Mom ran track, and Dad played basketball and baseball. They both got up super early to work out every morning—they were fanatics about it. They got me and Jim into sports when we were young, and they've been intense sports parents. Dad came to every game without fail, and Mom was a booster for both the basketball and football teams. She worked the Snack Shack at the games and organized the awards dinners at the end of the season. I honestly didn't know how she did it.

When I finished my chili, I put my bowl, plate, and silverware in the sink.

"It's still nice out," I said. "Can I bring Beth outside?"

"Sure," Mom said. "For a little while. Come in if it gets too cold."

The fall weather in Delaware was pretty mild, but it still got dark early, just like everywhere else. I turned on the floodlights on our back patio and wheeled Beth outside.

I hugged Beth again and held her hand. Then I closed my eyes, which I do sometimes when I'm with her, and imagined what it's like to be Beth. I could smell the fall leaves and feel the slightly cool air on my skin.

I opened my eyes. The breeze had picked up a stray leaf. It kissed Beth's cheek, and she smiled. I knew she was happy to be outside. Then it struck me, not for the first time, how happy Beth was most of the time.

And then I thought about how *unhappy* I had been all day. I kept complaining about how much I hated dancing, but I forgot how lucky I was to be able to move my feet. I was upset when Coach asked me to do extra drills in practice, but I forgot how lucky I was to be able to run and jump and shoot and play a sport I love.

Being with Beth always made me feel better.

She reminded me to take a deep breath and just be happy.

Beth grabbed my hand. *Sleep,* she signed.

Okay, I signed back, and I brought her back inside the house.

Tomorrow, when things get tough, be like Beth, I told myself.

A New Partner

"Of *course* I will go the mall with you today," Avery said, as we waited for homeroom to start the next morning. She took out her phone. "Let me text my mom."

"Thanks," I said.

"I guess I shouldn't be surprised that you don't have a dress yet," Avery said. "I got mine back in August, and that was pushing it. A lot of girls had claimed the best dresses already."

"What do you mean, 'claimed'?" I asked.

Avery tapped her phone. "There's a FaceChat

page set up for this year's cotillion," she said. "Whenever somebody gets a dress, they post it on the page. That way, you can make sure you don't have the same dress as anybody else."

"Seriously?" I asked. "What does it matter?"

"Of *course* it matters," Avery said. "You definitely don't want to show up in the same dress as somebody else. Then everyone will compare the two of you."

She started scrolling through the photos. "See? No two dresses the same." Then she stopped. "Here's mine. Isn't it cute?"

Avery held up the phone so I could see the picture. She was posing in front of a mirror in a sleeveless red dress with lace on the top and kind of a puffy skirt.

"I saw this adorable pink dress, but it was two inches above the knee," she told me. "And that's against cotillion rules."

"There are rules?" I asked, once again in disbelief.

Avery nodded. "Girls' dresses have to be one inch below the knee. They didn't used to allow sleeveless dresses, but they changed the rule a few years ago."

"Well, I want sleeves," I said, looking at Avery's exposed neck and shoulders in the photo. She looked great, but I couldn't imagine dancing around in a dress like that. "I *definitely* want sleeves."

"There are lots of cute dresses with sleeves," Avery promised, and then the bell rang.

"Avery, put the phone away please," Ms. Ebear said.

"Sorry, Ms. Ebear," Avery said. "It's school-related, though. I'm showing Elle the cotillion dresses."

A bunch of girls started talking excitedly when Avery said that. Ms. Ebear rolled her eyes.

"I have an opinion about that event that I am not allowed to express in class," she said, and from the way she said it you could tell that she didn't like the cotillion either. And that's just one more reason why Ms. Ebear is the best.

Principal Lubin's voice came over the speakers.

"What did one autumn leaf say to the other? I'm *falling* for you," he said. "And I'm falling for our

Spring Meadow basketball teams. See you all at the pep rally tomorrow!"

Ms. Ebear took attendance. "No Dylan? No Alex? No Colette?" she asked, frowning, and then looked down at her desk. "Looks like there's a cold going around."

"Your dance partner is missing," Avery whispered to me, and once again I felt a surge of hope. I couldn't dance without a partner, could I? I mean, I felt bad that Alex was sick, but I was definitely relieved that I wouldn't have to dance with him.

I figured I'd be sitting on the bleachers during gym. But when I got to gym, Mr. Patel had another idea.

"Elle and Amanda, your partners are not here," he said. "So you two can practice with each other today."

Amanda looked as surprised as I was, but we took our places in the line of dancers, facing each other.

"Elle, since you're the taller one, you lead," Mr. Patel told us.

Amanda and I got into dancing position. I held her right hand with my left, and put my right hand on her shoulder blade.

"I don't know if I can lead," I whispered to Amanda. "I really have no idea what I'm doing."

"Just try it. You'll be fine," she assured me with a smile.

"Let's begin with the box step," Mr. Patel said. "And then we'll add the flourishes we learned yesterday. Forward, side, together . . ."

This time, I started off with my left foot. I focused on the moves. It was actually easier being the one to lead, because I got to set the pace.

"Let's see some turns," Mr. Patel said.

I turned as I did the box step, and Amanda and I started to dance across the gym floor. I felt comfortable enough to look up from my feet, and when I did, I saw Amanda smiling at me.

"You're doing great!" she said.

"Now let's see some flourishes!" Mr. Patel called out.

"What are flourishes?" I asked Amanda. I hadn't

been paying attention to that yesterday, I'd been so busy trying to learn the steps.

"Don't worry, I've got it," Amanda said. Still holding my hand, she let go of my shoulder and twirled out to the right side. Then she twirled back in.

"Nice!" I said.

"Very good, everyone!" Mr. Patel said. "Now let's add some music."

He pressed the screen of a phone connected to a speaker on the sidelines, and some classical music came on.

"Freestyle for now," he instructed. "Move along with the beat. Then we're going to learn the routine that you'll all be doing at the cotillion."

I'm not going to say that I suddenly became a great dancer, but it was definitely much easier for me to lead. I didn't crash into anybody. And the best thing was that I was super relaxed to be dancing with Amanda.

We danced past Blake and Bianca.

"Hey, Elle!" Blake said cheerfully.

Bianca studied me and Amanda for a minute.

"You know, Elle, it's too bad we're not dancing the robot at the cotillion," she said.

I could tell she was setting me up for an insult, but I went for it anyway.

"Why?" I asked.

"Because you are so stiff," she replied. "You'd be great at it."

From the corner of my eye I saw Amanda roll hers, and I led her away to another part of the gym.

"Bianca is strange," Amanda said. "She can be so nice sometimes, and other times she can be so mean."

"She's had it in for me ever since Coach Ramirez decided to start me as center," I told her.

Amanda shrugged. "She shouldn't be surprised. I mean, you're the tallest. It makes total sense for you to play center."

"Yeah, I guess," I said.

"Anyway, you're not a stiff dancer," Amanda said. She smiled. "Let's try another flourish."

Holding hands, we twirled out from each other, then swirled back in so that we were facing each other. Then, cracking up, we twirled out again.

I couldn't believe it. I was actually having *fun* dancing. I wondered what would happen if Dylan and Alex didn't get over their colds. Would Amanda and I get to dance together at the cotillion?

I knew it was too much to hope for, but the thought made me happy. Getting to dance with Amanda would almost—*almost*—make wearing a stupid dress worth it.

Fashion Freak-Out

We should start at Belle's Boutique on the second floor," Avery was saying as we walked up to the mall entrance with my mom later that afternoon. "They don't have a huge selection, but the dresses there are definitely the cutest. If we don't find anything, we can go to Formals Inc. on the first floor."

"I'm glad Elle asked you to come with us, Avery," Mom said with a smile. "I have to confess, I haven't had to shop for a fancy dress for Elle in quite some time. I wouldn't know where to start."

I was walking behind the two of them, sulking, as they chatted away about dresses. We were at the Colonial Mall, a big mall just outside Wilmington. It had restaurants, a food court, a movie theater, a big department store on one end, and lots of smaller shops that sold everything you could imagine.

We hadn't gotten far inside the mall when Mom stopped in front of Kids Unlimited, a store that sold clothes for little kids.

"Oh, how cute," she said. "It was so much fun buying clothes for you kids when you were little, Elle. I do miss that."

I looked at the display of kid mannequins dressed up in fall clothes, wearing backpacks, and surrounded by fall leaves. The boys were wearing blue jeans, flannel shirts, and jackets with football emblems on them. The girls' clothes were pink and purple, and they wore leggings with lace on the bottom and shirts with ruffles at the hem and on the cuffs. One of the girls had on skinny jeans and a denim jacket, over a T-shirt that said "Princess" on it.

The whole display made me angry. "Look at

that!" I said. "The boys' clothes are loose fitting, and the girls' clothes are tight and they all have frills and ruffles and lacy stuff. And why do girls' shirts always say 'Princess'? Boys' shirts never say 'Prince.'"

"I see what you mean," Avery said, "but I like lace and frilly stuff."

"Right, but not *all* girls do," I said. "I never did."

Mom nodded. "That's true. I remember trying to put a lacy dress on you when you were two years old and you cried and screamed."

"I'm just saying," I argued. "There should be more choices."

"You know, I was reading a fashion blog about a new clothing company that's making girls' clothes with dinosaurs and planets and stuff," Avery said. "Maybe it will be a trend."

"I hope so," I said.

We kept walking, and soon it was my turn to stop in my tracks. The Sports Locker store had a display of basketball shoes in the front. I ran to it.

"Oh my gosh, the new Top Performance line is out!" I cried, picking one up. "Mom, look!"

"Elle, we just got you a new pair of shoes," Mom reminded me.

"But these have superior bounce," I told her. "I read this whole article about them, and they did scientific testing, and . . ."

"We are here to get you a dress," Mom interrupted me. "And maybe some new clothes to replace the rags you've been wearing."

I looked down at my "Greenmont Parks & Rec" sweatshirt, a hand-me-down from Jim.

"This is not a rag. This is an awesome sweatshirt," I said.

Avery grabbed my arm. "Come on, we need to go up this escalator," she said.

Mom and I followed Avery up the escalator to a small shop with fancy dresses in the window. A white sign with purple lettering read BELLE'S BOUTIQUE.

Inside, soft music played in the background. The dresses were hung up on neat racks around the store.

A woman walked up to us, wearing a black suit with a short skirt. Her blond hair was piled on top of her head.

"Can I help you?" she asked, smiling at Avery. She spoke with a Russian accent.

"Yes, my friend needs a semiformal dress for a cotillion," Avery replied, pointing to me.

The woman looked at me and her smile faded. She raised an eyebrow. "Your friend is very tall."

"Like a *model*, right?" Avery asked. "She's going to look gorgeous in one of your dresses."

The woman shook her head. "Not like a model. She is too tall for a model," she said, and I had a vague feeling I was supposed to be insulted by that. "I am Marina. I will find you a dress."

We followed her to a rack where she pulled out a sleeveless white dress with a puffy skirt. I was horrified.

"I definitely want sleeves," I said.

Marina frowned. She moved to another rack and took out a blue dress that was straight across the top, with the two tiniest sleeves I have ever seen.

"Are you kidding? Do those count as sleeves?" I asked.

"Just try it on, Elle," Avery said.

I took the dress and went to the dressing room. The top part fit, but the skirt was ridiculously short on me! It barely covered my underwear!

"Let's see, Elle," Mom said.

"Do I have to?" I asked.

"Yes, please," Mom replied.

With a heavy sigh, I stepped out of the dressing room. Mom clapped her hand over her mouth.

"It's too short," I said.

"Yes, definitely," Mom agreed. She turned to Marina. "Maybe something floor-length would be better for Elle?"

Marina nodded and came back with a sleeveless pale pink dress with a long skirt.

"No sleeves," I said flatly.

"Oh, but it's so pretty!" Avery said. "Just try it on, please?"

I tried on the dress and looked in the mirror. My shoulders and arms were completely bare. I felt naked! And the dress didn't even hit my ankles. It hit a few inches above them, and looked really weird.

I walked out of the dressing room. "No way,"

I said. "Seriously, I need sleeves. And it's still too short!"

"I will try mother of the bride section," Marina said.

"Mother of the bride?" I asked with a groan.

"I don't have a good feeling about this," Avery said.

Avery was right. Marina came back with a burgundy dress with sequins on the front. But it did have sleeves, and the bottom was long and flowy.

I tried it on. It fit okay, but when I looked in the mirror, I cringed.

"I look like a giant cranberry," I announced when I stepped out of the dressing room.

Mom frowned. "Well, this is a little mature for you."

Marina threw up her hands. "I do not think we have what she wants. You should go somewhere else."

Mom's eyebrows raised. "Yes, we will," she snapped. "Elle, get changed please."

I quickly changed and we headed back out into the mall.

"She was very rude," Mom said.

"Sorry, Ms. Deluca," Avery apologized. "She was nice to me when I was trying on dresses there."

"That's because you look great in everything," I mumbled.

"Elle, you are going to look gorgeous!" Avery promised. "Let's go to Formals Inc. They have so many cool dresses there. I'm sure we'll find you something."

"And when, exactly, does this get fun?" I asked.

"Just try to lighten up, please, Elle," Mom said.

I remembered my advice to myself: *Be like Beth.* I took a deep breath.

"Okay, let's do this," I said.

Formals Inc. turned out to be an enormous shop with pop music blaring. It was filled with girls looking at dresses on round racks.

"Okay, here's the plan," Avery said. "You get a dressing room. Your mom and I will find dresses and bring them to you to try on."

I walked to a dressing room and waited, killing the time by looking at basketball shoes on my phone. Then Mom and Avery showed up, their arms filled with dresses.

"Whoa," I said, gazing at the pile. "That's a lot of pink."

"You look beautiful in pink, with your blond hair," Mom said. "It suits you. Just give some of these dresses a chance."

"Fine," I said.

I tried on the first dress. It had pink puffy sleeves and the skirt was super short—again.

"No," I said flatly, stepping out of the dressing room quickly and then ducking back inside.

The next one had a flouncy skirt and tiny ruffles for sleeves. The skirt was too short again, and I looked ridiculous.

"These dresses all look like doll clothes on me," I complained.

Avery thrust a shimmery silver dress into my hands. "Try this one."

This dress was long and straight, at least, with wide shoulder straps. But it clung tightly to my body, which I did not like one bit.

"Absolutely not," I said, stepping out of the dressing room.

"Oh, I think it looks cool!" Avery said.

I stuck out my leg. "It's too tight. And it doesn't even hit my ankles. Everything is going to be too short!"

"Oh Elle, we'll find the perfect one," Avery said patiently. "The dresses really are pretty, and when you find one that fits, you'll look like a supermodel."

"I don't *want* to look like a supermodel!" I shot back. "I don't want a dress! And I especially don't even want to go to the cotillion!"

"Elle," Mom said in her warning voice, and I went back into the dressing room, holding back tears.

Whatever thoughts I had about being patient and happy and cool with the whole dress thing were gone. Mom and Avery shoved dress after dress into the room. Each one was lacy, or flouncy, or had sequins. And each one looked ridiculous on my body.

"How about this one?" Avery asked, handing me another white dress with a short skirt.

I took it without a word and stared at it. I knew

it would be no use trying it on. I'd had it.

I quickly slipped on my sweatshirt and jeans and opened the dressing room door. Mom looked surprised.

"Elle, we—"

"I'm done," I said.

"But Elle—"

"I'm DONE!" I said loudly, and a bunch of girls nearby turned to look at me strangely. Humiliated, I ran right out of the store.

It felt good to run. I ran and ran and didn't stop until I reached one of the mall exits. I hesitated before running outside.

Then I heard the sound of dogs barking. I turned to see that I was standing in front of The Pets Place. A big sign in the window announced: ADOPTION EVENT TODAY.

Curious, I stepped inside. A metal pen had been set up in the center of the store, and a bunch of dogs were running and playing inside. Volunteers wearing "Greenmont Animal Shelter" shirts were supervising the dogs.

I had always loved dogs, but Mom and Dad thought our lives were too complicated for pets. Avery had a poodle named Peanut who was so adorable and always ran up to me and did this cute little dance when I visited Avery's house. Every time I saw Peanut, I wished I had a dog of my own.

I walked up to the pen and a fluffy little brown dog ran up and jumped to greet me. I petted the top of his head. A gray dog came up next, and I petted her too.

Then the biggest dog I had ever seen barreled between both of them. This dog had short gray fur with white around his long, sad snout. His ears drooped, and soulful eyes gazed at me from his sweet face.

"Whoa, you're a big boy, aren't you?" I asked, petting him.

One of the volunteers approached me. "We call him Max," she said. "He's a Great Dane. Like Scooby Doo."

"Hi, Max," I said, rubbing his head. "Good boy."

Max got excited and stood up on his hind legs,

putting his paws on my shoulders. He was so tall that his face was right in my face.

I laughed. "Easy now," I said.

"He's a sweetheart," the volunteer said. "And he's been waiting for his forever family for a while. But he's just so big, he doesn't seem to fit with anybody."

I looked at Max's sweet face.

I know how you feel, Max! I thought.

When Will This All Be Over?

lle!" I heard my mom's voice behind me and spun around. Avery was with her.

"Uh, hi," I said, still embarrassed that I had run off.

"Ooh, what a cute dog!" Avery said, coming up to pet Max.

"He's a Great Dane," I said. Then I looked at Mom. "Hey, how about this: Why don't we adopt this dog instead of buying a dress that I'm never going to wear again?"

Mom sighed. "Elle, I know this is hard for you. I

do. But please, come back to the store with us so we can find you a dress."

"I still don't understand why I can't wear shorts, like in gym," I said. "Or even Jim's old suit."

"The rules are very specific," Mom replied. "It's just for a few hours, and it's for a grade. So I need you to put the same effort into this dance that you would with any other class or sport—and that means wearing a dress."

"But none of those dresses looked right," I complained. "They didn't even fit."

"Let's take one more look," Mom said. "I promise we won't find anything too frilly or uncomfortable."

"Fine," I said reluctantly.

When we got back to Formals Inc., one of the salesgirls walked up to us. She had freckles, which reminded me a little bit of Amanda. The name tag on her shirt read KRISTEN. She smiled at me.

"I saw you run out before," she said. "Dress stress?"

I nodded.

"I get it," she said. "But we have a lot of dresses

here, so I'm pretty sure we can find the perfect one for you. What exactly are you looking for?"

"Pants," I replied.

"But that is not an option," Mom said quickly.

Kristen nodded. "So, I'm thinking plain, no lace, no ruffles, right?"

"Right," I said.

"What about sleeves?" she asked.

I pointed to a spot halfway between my shoulder and my elbow.

"Got it," Kristen said. "And length?"

Mom replied for me. "It has to be below the knee," she said. "But the floor-length dresses are all too short for her."

"So something three-quarter," Kristen said thoughtfully. "I think I know just the dress."

She ran off and came back with a white dress with a pattern of red flowers and green leaves on it. I wasn't crazy about that, but the dress had no lace or no ruffles. It had normal, short sleeves.

"I'll try it," I said.

I went back into the dressing room and tried on

the dress. Surprisingly, it had pockets in the front! I slipped my hands in them, and it reminded me of my sweatshirt.

I studied the dress. It didn't itch. It had sleeves. And the skirt hit a few inches below my knee, so it looked normal.

I stepped outside the dressing room.

"Oh, Elle, that's so pretty!" Mom cried.

"Very retro," Avery said. "I love it."

"Well, I don't love the flowers," I said. "But it fits okay."

"Does that mean you'll take it?" Mom asked hopefully.

I definitely didn't want to try on any other dresses. "Yes," I said reluctantly.

Mom hugged me. "Oh, Elle, good for you! Now we just need to get you some shoes."

"Flats," I said immediately, and Avery laughed.

I looked at Kristen. "Thanks," I said.

"No problem, Elle," she said. "You look great."

I didn't feel like I looked great, so I quickly changed back into my sweatshirt and jeans. After

Mom paid for the dress we went to the shoe store, and we got out of there fast because I picked up plain white flats.

"I won't torture you any more today," Mom said, when she'd paid for the shoes. "No more clothes shopping. I need to get home and start dinner."

I turned to Avery. "Thanks for doing this with me."

"No problem," she said. "And don't worry. In two days, this will all be over."

"Two days?" I said. "That sounds like forever."

The next day, both Dylan and Alex were recovered from their colds and back in school, so any crazy idea I had of getting to dance with Amanda at the cotillion was dashed. And then Mr. Patel had another surprise for me.

"Dylan, you and Elle are partners again," the gym teacher said without explanation—but I had a suspicion that Alex had complained about me. I was starting to feel like I had the cooties or something.

At least Dylan didn't look disappointed when he

faced me. And when we started dancing, he was way more patient and nice than Alex had been. I couldn't help thinking about some of the dresses I'd tried on the day before—some of them would have looked nice on me, but they were too short. That was kind of like Dylan. If he were taller, we might have been able to dance okay together.

Mr. Patel put on the music again, and I plowed through the dance practice as best as I could. He had a fairly simple routine worked out for us. Box step, box step, turn, turn, box step, box step, turn, turn, flourish. Repeat. I knew what I was *supposed* to be doing.

Doing it was another matter. I was back to being the follower, not the leader, and I got confused all over again. I kept stepping on poor Dylan's feet. And we bumped into other couples twice. I was so glad when gym class was over.

The rest of the day went by quickly, because everyone was excited about the pep rally. After seventh period we all filed into the gym. We basketball players had changed into our uniforms, and everyone else was wearing Spring Meadow School spirit wear—T-shirts and hats, mostly, although some kids had actually painted their faces with yellow and green stripes.

Principal Lubin loved pep rallies, so we had one at the start of the football season, soccer season, basketball season, and track season. The pep rallies were for every team in the school, from the pee wee teams to the high school varsity team. That's a lot of teams, and a lot of players, so to keep things simple, the pep rally pretty much consisted of the marching band playing songs and everyone cheering along.

Principal Lubin approached the microphone, gazing at the crowd through his wire-rimmed glasses. Today he was wearing a green jacket, green pants, a green shirt, and a bright yellow tie to show his school spirit.

"Good afternoon, students!" he said, and everybody quieted down. "There's a lot of pep in this room already. Good job! Now put your hands together for the Spring Meadow marching band and cheerleaders!"

The marching band entered in their green and

yellow uniforms and started playing, "Rah Rah Spring Meadow!" The high school cheerleaders entered through an opposite door and started cartwheeling across the floor. Everybody in the stands jumped to their feet.

"Rah Rah Spring Meadow!" we yelled along with the cheerleaders.

I was standing in the bleachers with my basketball friends, Avery, Hannah, Natalie, and Caroline. We put our arms around one another's shoulders as we joined in with the cheers.

"Basketball girl squad!" Hannah yelled out over the music.

The band played a few more songs, the cheerleaders jumped and flipped, and by the end we were all stomping our feet and clapping. When it was over, I was pumped for practice.

Yes, I was still getting comfortable in the court in my new body. Yes, I was nervous about playing center. But this was basketball, not dancing. I knew how to conquer it. I knew how to get better at it. It was in my blood.

"The Nighthawks are in for a great season!" Principal Lubin cheered as the last song died down. "Have a great night everybody, and we'll see you at the cotillion tomorrow!"

"Woo hoo!" I whooped, as everyone in the school scrambled down from the bleachers. I had my duffel with me, and ran into the locker room to get changed.

At practice, Coach Ramirez saw how pumped we were, so after we warmed up she launched us into a practice game, with the same sides as last time.

I was ready. When Coach threw up the first toss, I jumped up and *slammed* that ball toward Avery. It felt good.

And then I fell forward and crashed into Bianca.

"Watch the fouls, Deluca!" Coach Ramirez yelled.

That bothered me, and I tried to shake it off. But when I got control of the ball I had a clear shot near the free throw line, and I missed. The ball bounced off the right side of the backboard.

Do not psych yourself out! I thought.

I pushed hard during that practice game. I made

six shots. But I missed even more than that. And I accidentally fouled Tiff, who got to take a foul shot and got an extra point for her team.

I expected Coach Ramirez to ride me, but to be honest, she spent most of her time yelling at Patrice.

"Patrice, look alive out there!"

"Patrice, you've got better form than that!"

"Patrice, that rebound was *yours*! You should have grabbed it!"

When the practice game ended, Bianca's team won by two points, and I couldn't help feeling that my foul against Tiff was responsible for our team's loss. Coach Ramirez had us sit on the bleachers before she dismissed us.

"Sunday's game is going to set the tone for the season," she said. "I know we can win, but I'm going to need more from you."

"Yes, Coach!" we all replied.

She looked at me. "Elle, if you're going to be center on this team, I need you to be scoring more. Go after those rebounds. And try to be aware of your form when you're shooting."

"Yes, Coach," I replied quietly. I waited for her to dress down the rest of the players.

She didn't.

"Okay, that's it for today," Coach said. "See you on Sunday."

I wasn't feeling very talkative as we headed back to the locker room. I had a sinking feeling in my stomach.

This wasn't like failing in dancing. This was *basketball*. I couldn't fail in basketball. I was working hard. I was giving it my all. But was it my fault that my brain and body had stopped working together?

I was dreading the weekend. Tomorrow, I had to dance in front of the whole school. And Sunday, well, it felt like my whole future in basketball was riding on that one game.

Dancing the Night Away

The next morning, after breakfast, I put on my basketball shorts, my new shoes, and a T-shirt, and headed outside to the basketball hoop in the driveway. I practiced all morning. I practiced layups and foul shouts. I practiced dribbling and defensive slides. After lunch I went for a run, and then I practiced some more.

Mom came out to the driveway at two o'clock. "Elle, you need to get ready for the cotillion," she said.

"But it's not until five o'clock!" I argued.

"We have to be there at five," Mom said, "and you need to shower, and wash your hair, and . . ."

"Okay, okay," I grumbled, and I took one last shot at the basket before I went in.

Swish!

After I showered, Mom made me use a blow dryer on my hair, which is a pain. My hair is long and it's so much easier to just put it in a ponytail and let it dry naturally. But Mom was in control of my pre-cotillion routine, and I had to go with it.

She gave me a pair of stockings to wear with the dress. I hate wearing tights because they're so itchy! It took me twenty minutes to get them on because they kept rolling down every time I tried to pull them up. When I finally succeeded, they barely reached my waist—but just barely.

Ugh. I hated them. But I had no choice. Next I put on the dress, and then my white flats.

I looked in the mirror. I guess I looked okay. I mean, the dress looked nice. But I didn't look like *me*. And the stockings were already annoying me.

Then I noticed my basketball shorts on the floor

and I had an idea. I slipped them on under my dress, and the wide skirt of the dress didn't cling to them, so you couldn't tell I was wearing them. But *I* knew I was wearing them, and somehow, it made me feel better.

I walked into the hallway and bumped into Jim, who was dressed in a black suit, white shirt, and pink bowtie. His eyes went wide.

"Wow, Elle! You look like a movie star!" he said.

"Uh, thanks," I said. "You look nice too."

We walked into the living room, where Mom and Dad were sitting with Beth. Dad stood up when he saw us.

"Honey, you look beautiful!" he said. "You're going to be the *Elle* of the ball. Get it?"

I groaned. "Now you sound like Principal Lubin," I said. "But thanks."

I felt awkward. Why was everybody making such a big deal? I was the same person I always was, just in a different wrapping. Did wearing a fancy dress make you beautiful? Is that all that mattered?

"See, you made such a fuss over getting a dress

and you look great," Mom said. "Let me get a picture of the both of you. Go outside by the tree."

"The tree" was a big, shady maple tree on our front lawn. Every time Mom wanted a photo of us—first day of school, Halloween, dressed up for a wedding—we took it under the tree.

Jim and I walked to the tree and posed, smiling, as Mom took pictures. She put down the phone and I saw that she was a little weepy.

"Honestly, where does the time go?" she asked. "My little babies are growing up so fast!"

Dad put his arm around her. "Don't worry," he said. "They've got plenty more growing up to do."

"Yeah, well, I've got to go pick up Megan," Jim said, talking about his cotillion dance partner. "If this love fest is over, I'll meet you guys there."

Big gatherings can be tough for Beth, so she was staying home with the babysitter. I gave her a hug good-bye and then climbed into the backseat of the family van.

"Are you feeling excited at all about the dance?" Mom asked, turning around to talk to me.

"Not really," I said. "I'm more excited about tomorrow's game. Are we going to have spaghetti when I get home?"

"No, Elle, we'll be eating at the cotillion," Mom said. "You remember. The school serves sandwiches and fruit."

"But you *know* I need to eat Italian food the night before a game," I said. "It's . . . it's my thing."

I didn't like to eat a lot the morning of a big game. But the night before, I ate Italian food— spaghetti and meatballs, pizza, lasagna, whatever Mom or Dad made. And then I used that energy for the game the next day. I'm sure it's not scientific, but that's what I had been doing since fifth grade, and it worked for me.

"Next time, Elle, I promise," Mom said.

I sulked the whole way to the school. The cotillion was ruining everything.

When we arrived, the parking lot was packed with cars and we had to find a spot along the road. Boys in suits and girls in fancy dresses walked across the school grounds to the entrance of the gym.

I'd been to cotillions before to watch Jim dance, so I knew what to expect. Orange, yellow, and red streamers hung from the gym ceiling, and on each side of the gym, jars of fall flowers decorated tables covered in white tablecloths.

Principal Lubin was already standing at a microphone.

"Good afternoon, everyone!" he said. "I'm *falling* in love with our fall weather, aren't you?"

My dad started cracking up. He loved Principal Lubin's jokes.

"Seventh graders, please report to Mr. Patel," Principal Lubin continued. "The dancing begins in ten minutes!"

Mom hugged me. "You're going to do great, Elle," she promised.

"Uh huh," I said. My palms were starting to sweat. I couldn't wait for the whole dumb dance to be over!

I walked over to where the seventh graders were gathering and saw Avery.

"Elle, you look great!" she said, hugging me.

"Thanks," I replied. "So do you. You were born to wear that dress."

It was true. Avery looked better in her red dress than she had in the picture. Her braids were coiled up on top of her head. She looked amazing. But what's more, Avery looked like *Avery*. She loved dressing up, and her face was glowing with confidence.

Out of the corner of my eye I spotted Amanda. She looked really cute in a white dress with little red flowers on it. Then it hit me—we were wearing the same dress!

She caught my eye and must have guessed from the expression on my face what I was thinking, because she starting laughing and walked up to me.

"Nice dress," she said.

"Well, it looks nice on *you*," I said. "I'm not too crazy about it."

Amanda slipped her hands into the pockets. "I got it because of these."

I grinned. "Yeah, the pockets are awesome!"

"I guess you two didn't check out the FaceChat page."

We both turned at the sound of Bianca's voice.

"Nope," I said.

"Yeah, me neither," said Amanda.

"Too bad," Bianca said. "Then you could have avoided wearing the same dress."

"Why would we want to do that?" Amanda asked.

"Because—" Bianca hesitated. "Because it's just, you know, you shouldn't."

"I didn't see that in the rules," I said.

"And we can't help it if we both have the same awesome taste," Amanda added.

Bianca rolled her eyes. "Whatever makes you happy," she said, and then she walked away.

Mr. Patel appeared. "All right, everyone. Line up with your partners."

I scanned the group and found Dylan. He smiled when he saw me.

"Wow, Elle, you look nice," he said.

"So do you," I told him.

We followed Mr. Patel's instructions and lined up on the gym floor, just like we had in practice. I tried to block out the rows and rows of eyes watching us from the bleachers.

"Presenting the seventh grade class of Spring Meadow School," Principal Lubin announced. "Let the dancing begin!"

The music began to play, and we started to dance. Box step. Box step. Turn. Turn. Box step. Box step. Turn. Turn. Flourish. Repeat.

I moved my arms and legs stiffly, but I got all the steps right. I kept my eyes focused on the top of Dylan's hand. My hands got super sweaty, but I didn't stop to wipe them on my nice dress, like I was dying to. And best of all, we didn't bump into anybody.

Then the music stopped. We had been dancing for less than five minutes, and now it was over. Relief washed over me like a tidal wave.

"Let's give a big hand to our seventh graders!" Mr. Lubin cheered. "Dancers, please find a seat in the bleachers."

Avery grabbed my arm as we headed off the gym

floor. "Come to the bathroom with me," she said.

"Sure," I said, confused. As we walked she grabbed a small duffel from the side of the bleachers.

"What's up?" I asked her.

Avery didn't say anything until we got to the bathroom. Then she pulled something out of the bag. "Here, you can wear this for the rest of the night."

She held up a sparkly white hoodie. I laughed.

"It's perfect!" I cried, and then I put it on and let out a long breath. "Now I definitely feel more like myself. Thank you."

We hurried back to the bleachers to watch the other dancers. In practice, I had spent most of the time looking at my feet or Dylan's head, so I hadn't really paid attention to anybody else. As the eighth graders were dancing, I could see that some kids— boys and girls—looked just as uncomfortable as I had felt. And one boy kept stepping on his partner's feet, and a girl kept wiping her sweaty hands on her dress.

I watched the dancers in each grade carefully, and I noticed the same thing every time. Some kids looked like they loved it, while others looked miserable. And every group had kids who made mistakes.

Then it was time for the seniors to dance, and Jim got on the floor with his friend Megan.

"It's Jim!" I cried, nudging Avery, and we began clapping like crazy.

The seniors' dance was way fancier than our seventh grade dance. As Jim and Megan whirled and twirled and dipped across the dance floor, I realized how hard he had worked to get that good. And I was really proud of him.

When the dance finished, I launched to my feet.

"Yay Jim! Yay Megan! Woo hoo!"

"A big hand for our seniors," Principal Lubin said. "This class is filled with some amazing dancers!"

Everyone cheered again.

"And now, all students are welcome to dance," Principal Lubin said. "Food will be served shortly."

"Are you going to dance?" Avery asked me. "You can dance with whoever you want now."

I glanced over at Amanda in the bleachers. For a

split second I thought about dancing with her, but I changed my mind.

"I think I am done with dancing," I said.

But then Blake walked up and did a goofy bow in front of me.

"May I have this dance, Elle?" he asked.

"Are you serious?" I replied.

"I am always serious," Blake said, wiggling his eyebrows.

I shook my head. "Well, I guess I can't say no."

Blake led me out onto the dance floor. Waltz music was still playing, so we just moved in a simple box step, over and over.

"You know you're the only person who could get me back on this dance floor, right?" I asked.

"I figured," Blake said. "Anyway, thanks for dancing with me. I think Bianca wanted me to keep dancing with her, and well, I just needed a Bianca break."

I nodded. "I know what you mean."

Suddenly the music stopped. I looked over by the speakers and one of the senior boys was plugging a phone into them.

Loud music started blaring through the gym. The song "Don't Stop Trying," was playing—it's the song that plays during warm-ups before every basketball game.

Every basketball player in the room started shrieking with happiness. I let go of Blake's hand as Avery ran onto the gym floor with Amanda, Hannah, Natalie, and the rest of our team. We started jumping up and down and singing along.

Principal Lubin approached the senior by the speakers, and they must have come to an agreement because the kid deejayed with his phone for the rest of the night. Nobody had to dance with a partner— we just jumped around and shook our heads up and down and had fun. I even kind of liked the way my skirt twirled around me when I jumped.

I danced with Avery and Blake and Natalie, and at one point Avery got out her phone and pushed me and Amanda together.

"I need a picture of the twins," she said, and we made a silly pose, doing peace signs when Avery snapped the shot.

I was having so much fun that I was actually disappointed when Mom walked up and said it was time to go home.

"Big day tomorrow, Elle," Mom said. "Don't forget about your game."

"How could I forget?" I asked.

I said good-bye to everybody and headed back to the car with Mom and Dad.

"You did a wonderful job, Elle," Mom said, as we pulled out of the parking lot. "But I think I finally understand how uncomfortable you were, once I saw the look on your face. And you weren't the only one."

I nodded. "Yeah, I know." It felt good, though, to know that Mom finally seemed to understand how I felt.

While we were talking, Dad pulled in to Sal's Pizzeria, which was a few blocks away from the school.

"What are we doing?" I asked.

Dad turned and smiled. "Italian food. Those cucumber sandwiches didn't fill me up, and I bet they didn't fill you up, did they?"

I shook my head and smiled at him gratefully. A little while later I was eating a bowl of spaghetti and mulling over the night.

The dance was over. It hadn't been a disaster. It had even been kind of fun.

But I still had one worry: Tomorrow was the opening game of the season.

I had to nail it.

The Runaway Train

W hen I started getting serious about basketball last year, I researched the pregame routines of WNBA players. Some of them are too superstitious to even talk about them. But most of them say the same thing: They do a shootaround. Then they eat a very light meal. Then they nap or meditate. After that, some of them listen to music to get pumped up.

This year, all our Sunday games were at 11:30 a.m., with a gym report time of 11:00 a.m. Squeezing in all of those activities would be tricky, but I was determined to try it out.

Here is what I did the morning of our first game of the season:

7:00 a.m.: woke up

7:15–8:15: informal shootaround practice in the driveway

8:15–8:45: showered

8:45–9:15: ate half a bagel with peanut butter

9:15–10:15: napped (well, mostly laid on my bed with my eyes closed, but I tried)

10:15: got dressed for the game

I added my own personal routine to this part. I put on my jersey. Then I put on my socks and shoes. *Then* I put on my shorts, being sure to put my right foot through the leg of my shorts first. That's because I wanted to make sure I started off each game on the right foot. Get it?

At 10:30 we left for the game, which was being held at the middle school in North Creek, just a few towns away. I put in my headphones and listened to "Don't Stop Trying" from the dance the night before.

When we got to the gym at 10:50, I saw Bianca and Tiff were already there, warming up on one end of the court.

I couldn't say that I was happy to see Bianca. She hadn't exactly been friendly to me lately. But there was no room on a basketball team for infighting. We had to stick together and cooperate if we wanted to win.

"Hey Tiff," I said. "Hey B."

They both nodded to me. Tiff passed me the ball. I dribbled up to the hoop and took a shot.

Tiff got the rebound and dribbled up to me. "What do you think, Elle? Can we beat these guys?"

She nodded to the other side of the gym, where the North Creek Chargers were starting to warm up in their blue and white uniforms. Tiff was really competitive, and also a kind of math genius, and she liked to calculate our odds of winning and losing before each game.

Tiff didn't wait for me to answer. "We had a better record than them last year," she said. "But since this is the first game of the season I don't know if they've gotten any new players. I'm pretty sure that they don't have anybody as tall as you, though."

"Does that matter?" I asked.

"Of course it does," Tiff replied. "Statistically, anyway."

She passed the ball to me. I didn't know what to say. There was that pressure again—that just because I was the tallest, it meant I could play better than anyone else. And that simply wasn't true—especially when I thought about how many times I had messed up during practice that week.

The rest of the team arrived all at once then and joined us on the gym floor. Amanda walked up to me.

"Hey, we're wearing the same thing again!" she joked. "We have to stop doing that."

I smiled. "Well, I think it's okay at games."

Coach Ramirez strolled onto the court. "All right girls, line up! I want to see some layups."

We lined up and took turns doing layups, one after another. The bleachers started filling up with people. I could feel my energy building and building. . . .

"Nighthawks, huddle!" Coach Ramirez called out.

We quickly gathered in a circle.

"Elle, Bianca, Tiff, Patrice, Avery, you're my starters," Coach said. "Everybody else, be ready to go in when I call you. Don't get distracted."

"Yes, Coach!" we yelled.

"Stay focused, remember your position, and keep your eye on the ball!" Coach Ramirez said. "Let's do this!"

We gave a cheer and broke away from the circle. Amanda, Caroline, Dina, Natalie, and Hannah sat on the bench, while the rest of us took our positions on the court.

I stood in the center of the court and the Chargers center walked up to me. She was almost a foot shorter than I was, I guessed, but I didn't want to underestimate her.

The ref's whistle blew, and he tossed the ball in the air between us. I sprang up from my heels and batted it away.

It bounced to Patrice. She dribbled from side to side, hesitating.

"Move, Patrice!" Coach Ramirez yelled.

Then she passed it to Bianca. As Bianca took it over the center line, the ref's whistle blew.

"Back court violation!"

Patrice had kept the ball on the wrong side of the court for too long. Bianca tossed the ball to the player who had been guarding her, who moved to the sidelines to throw it in. I ran to my position under the basket.

The Chargers guard threw it to their center. I plucked it out of the air before she got it and dribbled down the court. The center caught up to me just as I jumped up to take my shot.

Somehow, my legs disobeyed me, and I ended up flat on my back with the ball still between my hands. The Chargers center grabbed it from me and took it down the court.

And that was pretty much the highlight of my game play during the first quarter—falling on my butt. Tiff and Bianca both managed to score in the two-point zone, and Avery made a gorgeous three-point shot that was beautiful to watch.

On the other side, the Chargers made a few successful shots. The girl guarding Patrice kept stealing the ball from her, so they had control more than we did. At the end of the quarter, the score was Nighthawks 7, Chargers 11.

Coach switched up some players for the second quarter. She put Hannah in for Bianca, and sent Natalie in to swap with Avery, but she left in me, Tiff, and Patrice.

The highlight of my second quarter: I stepped out of bounds not once, not twice, but three times. Every time I charged down the court, I just couldn't slow down or stop properly.

Thankfully, I managed to score two baskets from the three-point arc. After that, the Chargers put two girls on me, and one of them gave me an elbow in the hips the next time I tried to shoot. So I got two free throws out of it—and I made them both.

We had a five-minute break when the second quarter ended with a score of 18–18. Coach Ramirez was not happy with my out-of-bounds violations.

"Deluca, you're like a runaway train out there," she snapped at me during our half-time pep talk. "You've got to figure out when to stop. You're costing us points."

"Yes, Coach," I said. *Runaway train?* I saw Bianca smirk, and I prayed that wasn't going to become my new nickname.

She turned to Patrice. "They're taking the ball away from you like they're taking candy from a baby," she said. "You've got to think faster out there."

Patrice nodded. "Yes, M—Coach."

Coach clapped her hands. "All right. Bianca, I want you to play center this next quarter. Then I want to see Caroline, Amanda, Hannah, and Dina in there."

I knew Coach wasn't necessarily benching me because I was playing badly. There are rules in the league about how many consecutive quarters any one player can play. And I knew that if I was benched, it made sense for Bianca to play center. But I still felt a little pang of something that felt like jealousy.

I know, that didn't make sense, right? I had never wanted to play center in the first place. But now I was center, for better or worse, and I wanted to own it. I wanted to be good at it. No—I wanted to be the *best* at it.

On the bench, I kept my eyes on the court. It's amazing how fast an eight-minute quarter can go. I noticed a few things.

Dina was a much better forward than Patrice. She was more confident, and a better guard when she needed to be. So why did Coach Ramirez always start Patrice? Was it just because Patrice was her kid? But then if she was playing favorites with Patrice, why was she always yelling at her? I couldn't figure it out.

Then there was Caroline. She wasn't the fastest, or the best shooter. But on the court, I could see that she was intensely focused all the time and trying really hard. She never went out of bounds. She never forgot her position. She missed a few shot opportunities on the court, but when she got to do a free throw, she nailed it. I had never seen her look so happy.

Amanda was definitely not as confident, but this was her first game. Twice, she passed the ball when she shouldn't have, practically right into the hands of the Chargers. But near the end of the quarter she caught a rebound and made an awesome layup, and I was really happy for her.

The third quarter ended in a tie again, 24–24.

"Elle, Bianca, Tiff, Patrice, Avery!" Coach Ramirez called out. "Here!"

The five of us ran up to her.

"It's the fourth quarter, so we can go with a full-court press on these guys," she said. "You know what to do, right?"

"Yes, Coach!" we replied.

A full-court press is basically girl-to-girl defense, when instead of just covering members of the opposing team near their basket, you cover them all over the court. It's considered aggressive defense, so the league only allows you to do it in the fourth quarter.

I was back playing center, and made sure the Nighthawks had control of the ball from the start. Bianca took the ball across the center line and passed it to Patrice. She took a shot and missed, but I got the rebound and sank it for two points.

Bianca high-fived me, and we both smiled. The Chargers had the ball next, and we implemented our full-court press. I stuck with the Chargers center. She got the ball near the basket and crouched into shooting position. I lurched forward so I could pivot and turn with my back to her to get the rebound—but I lurched too far and my body slammed into her. The ref's whistle blew.

"Foul!"

The Chargers center got two shots—and made both of them. So it was like the two points I had scored didn't even count!

The next time the Nighthawks got control of the ball, Avery broke away and stampeded down the court with it. I ran like a rocket down the court after her, and once again ended up out of bounds.

"Runaway train!" Bianca called out.

I knew I had to stay focused. The next time the Chargers had the ball, I was waiting for the rebound when one of the players took the shot. It bounced high off the backboard, and my giraffe height came in handy—I grabbed it out of the air before anyone else could reach it. Then I sank the basket.

We were up, 28–26. But the Chargers had the ball again and even though our girl-to-girl defense was pretty tight, one of them made an amazing three-point shot that sailed into the basket.

Now we were down by a point. I glanced at the scoreboard and saw that the game was almost over. The quarter was going like lightning!

As the time ticked down, Avery passed the ball to me. I took it to the hoop and stopped, lining up my shot. I hadn't been paying too much attention to the Chargers center. She was fast, but she hadn't been able to block any of my shots so far.

But this girl must have been motivated, because she jumped up like she had rockets in her shoes and knocked the ball out of my hands! The ball skidded across the court, and players from both teams scrambled to get it.

Bianca got to it first. She jumped up and took her shot. The ball sank into the basket.

Two seconds later, the buzzer rang. The game was over, and we had won, 30–29!

We quickly formed a line and moved down the court, shaking hands with the Chargers. Then we broke away. Everyone was swarming around Bianca and chanting her name for making the winning basket.

I could have made that basket, I scolded myself. *I should have made that basket.*

Avery ran up and high-fived me.

"We did it!" she cheered. Then she looked at my face. "What's the matter?"

"Nothing," I said. "I mean, I'm glad we won, but . . ."

"But?" Avery asked.

"Well, I could have been the hero," I said. "But instead, I'm the runaway train!"

Freckles (or, Like Girl, Like Dog)

P izza! Pizza! Pizza!"

Bianca had suggested that we go for a post-game celebration, and now the whole team—including Coach Ramirez—was sitting around a bunch of tables pushed together at Sal's Pizzeria.

I had only eaten half a bagel that morning, and played three quarters of a basketball game, so I was ravenous. So was everyone else, which explains why we were chanting like a bunch of Amazons. I think we were also giddy from our win.

Coach handled the order: one plain, one sausage,

and one veggie pizza. We each had two slices that we devoured in minutes. Then there were two slices of plain left over.

"Who wants the extra slices?" Natalie called out.

Everyone raised their hand.

"We should give them to the game MVP," Hannah suggested.

"That's Bianca!" Dina cried. "She made the winning basket!"

Everyone cheered for that. How could we argue?

"Well, I only want one slice," Bianca said. "And I think Tiff deserves the other one."

Avery looked at me with a fake sad face. "Oh, well. Maybe next time," she whispered.

"It's okay. I want to go for a run after this anyway, and another slice would just weigh me down," I said. "You want to come?"

Avery shook her head. "I'm on big sister duty this afternoon," she replied. "I promised Addison that I'd help her with her diorama for Ms. Houston's class."

Avery's little sister was in second grade. We'd

both had Ms. Houston, too, and we'd both had to make dioramas for her. That's right—not one, but multiple.

"That teacher is diorama crazy," I said, shaking my head. "I don't understand. When in life will we ever be asked to make dioramas again?"

"I actually think they're kind of fun," Avery said. "Anyway, my mom told Addison that I'm a diorama expert, so I'm stuck."

"No problem," I said, and I texted Blake. You up for a run in 30?

Blake texted me back with an emoji of a little guy running.

So about a half hour later, I was wearing sweats and a T-shirt and jogging with Blake down our street, heading toward the park.

"So you won!" Blake said, after I told him. "That's great!"

"Yes and no," I answered, and then I told him about some of my more epic clumsy moves on the court. And my possible new nickname.

Blake grinned. "Runaway Train? That's not so

bad," he said, and then he sped up. "Come on, Runaway Train! Try and catch me!"

I quickly caught up to Blake and we kept the pace all the way to Greenmont Park. Because it was a sunny, beautiful fall day, the park was crowded. Teenagers tossed flying discs or played pickup games on the basketball court there. Little kids ran around, laughing and climbing in the playground. We started a loop around the park and soon came to the fenced-in dog park at the end.

"Elle!"

I turned at the sound of my name and saw Amanda behind us, walking a dog on a leash.

"Oh, hey!" I said, stopping, and Blake stopped too. "Is this your dog?"

I knelt down to pet the dog, who had white and brown fur, droopy brown ears, and brown spots all across her white snout.

"Yes," Amanda replied. "This is Freckles."

Blake petted the dog too. "What kind of dog is it?"

"She's an English springer spaniel," Amanda

explained. "We rescued her from a shelter in Virginia last year."

"I love her name," I said.

Amanda smiled. "It fits her, right?" she said. "She came with a different name when we got her, but we had to name her Freckles once we saw her."

"Of course," I said. "She's got great freckles, just like you."

"I actually used to hate my freckles," Amanda admitted, and I was surprised to hear that.

"Really?" I asked.

Amanda nodded. "I even looked online for ways to get rid of them," she said. "I tried rubbing lemon juice on them. It didn't work. But then, once we adopted Freckles . . . I realized they're not so bad."

"I get that," I said, standing up. "Well, have a good walk with Freckles!"

"Thanks!" Amanda replied with a smile.

Blake and I continued to loop around the park. The whole time, I thought about Max, the dog I had seen at the mall.

When I got home, the house smelled great. I

entered the kitchen and found Dad at the stove. Mom was chopping vegetables for a salad.

"Good run?" Mom asked.

"Awesome," I said, grabbing the water pitcher from the fridge. I looked at Dad. "What smells so good?"

"My famous chicken parm," Dad said. "I made a lot, so I hope you're hungry."

I nodded. "Definitely," I said. "So, in the park, Blake and I ran into Amanda—you know, from the team—and she was walking her dog. It got me thinking about that dog at the mall."

"You mean that big dog that Avery and I found you with?" Mom asked.

I nodded. "He's a Great Dane. I just . . . I know it's a lot of work to have a pet and everything, but if we *were* ever going to get a dog, I think he would be a great one."

"Why him?" Dad asked.

"Well, you know, he's supersized," I said, "just like me."

Mom and Dad gave each other a look. But I

didn't really think much about it. They had always been very clear that a dog was not a good idea for the Deluca family.

I ran upstairs to shower and change. Life was sure full of ups and downs, I thought. Sometimes you score, and sometimes you fall on your butt. Sometimes you get the extra slice of pizza, and sometimes you have to settle for just two.

Sometimes you get a dog—and sometimes, you just get chicken parm.

In the News

Read all about it! The newest online edition of the *Spring Meadow News* has been posted on the school website," Principal Lubin announced the next morning during homeroom. "Happy reading!"

I opened my laptop and clicked right over to the sports section. There was an article: "Seventh Grade Nighthawks Defeat Chargers in Nail Biter."

I scanned the article, which focused on Bianca's game-winning basket. Then I spotted my name.

"Elle Deluca is the tallest member of the team—

and probably taller than any other player the Night-hawks will face this year," the article said. "Her height will surely give this team the advantage as they move forward in the season."

Her height, I repeated in my head.

They didn't say anything about my playing abil-ity. Or the fact that I was a hard worker or a team player. Shouldn't those things count as much?

Frustrated, I closed my laptop. What was it my mom always said?

You can't control what people say or think about you. You can only control how you react to that. You can only control who you are.

It was up to me, then. If I wanted people to notice more than my height, I'd have to start playing better. And that had to start now.

Coach Ramirez had us do ball handling skills at practice, and I focused like I never had before. I was feeling pretty pumped up when practice ended— and a little surprised when Mom came to pick me up, and Dad and Jim were in the car with her.

"What's up?" I asked, sliding into the backseat.

"We just need to run a little errand together," Mom said, and she had a funny smile on her face.

I looked at Jim. "Tell me!"

Jim shrugged. "I seriously have no idea."

"Can't you give us a clue?" I asked my parents.

"Nope," Dad said, with the same mischievous grin on his face that Mom had.

"Oh, but I do have something I can tell you, Elle," Mom said. "I talked to the school this morning about the cotillion, and how the rules make some kids uncomfortable. Principal Lubin agreed. He said he's heard from a few other parents, too, and he and the school board have considered making some changes."

"Like what?" I asked.

"Well, everyone still has to wear formal wear, but girls will no longer be required to wear dresses," Mom replied. "And they are considering allowing friends to dance together, whether they're boys or girls."

"Yes!" I cheered. "Thanks for talking to him, Mom."

I pictured myself dancing with Blake or Avery or even Amanda. I got so lost in thought that I forgot we were running a mysterious errand. So when Mom pulled up in front of the Greenmont Animal Shelter, I was surprised.

"What are we doing here?" I asked. I had an idea, but no . . . it couldn't be, could it?

We all got out of the car. When we reached the entrance, Mom and Dad stopped and looked at us.

"So, your dad and I had a long talk last night," Mom said. "We had already been thinking that now that you kids are older, a dog might be good for this family. But we weren't sure how to start finding one."

"Then Elle told us about the Great Dane here," Dad said. "Your Mom called this morning and filled out the application. They called back a few hours later and said we were accepted."

I could feel happy tears welling up in my eyes.

"You mean . . . ," I said.

Mom nodded. "He's coming home with us."

She opened the door and we stepped inside. One

of the shelter volunteers had Max the Great Dane on a leash. When he saw me, he jumped up and put his paws on my shoulders again.

"I think he remembers me!" I said.

The volunteer smiled. "We're so glad he found a good home," she said. "Max is one of our favorites here."

"Do we have to call him Max?" I asked. "I mean, he doesn't exactly look like a Max."

"You can call him whatever you like," the volunteer replied.

Ever since I'd decided I wanted a dog, I had the perfect name picked out. "How about Zobe?" I asked.

Zobe started to lick my face, so I took that as a "yes." "He likes it!" I said.

Dad hugged the dog. "Welcome to the family, Zobe," he said.

"This is a pretty cool dog," Jim said. "I've wanted one since I was a kid. I can't believe you caved for Elle!"

"The time was right, Jim," Mom said. "Anyway, you can enjoy him too."

"Can we bring him home now?" I asked. "Beth is going to love him!"

"Your parents just need to fill out some paper-work, and Zobe is all yours," the volunteer replied.

She handed me Zobe's leash.

"Come on, Zobe. Let's go outside and wait!" I said.

I took Zobe onto the lawn outside the shelter and he got so excited that he jumped on me again, knocking me down. I laughed.

It felt great to have another too-tall member of the family. Zobe was supersized like me. He was clumsy and a little bit goofy. But that didn't bother Zobe at all. He was happy just being Zobe.

If Zobe was happy being Zobe, then why couldn't I be happy being me—tall, clumsy, and a little bit goofy me? Yes, I was unusually tall. But my height wasn't the only thing that defined me. I knew there were a lot more things that made me the person I am. And it was up to me to share those things with the world.

"All done," Mom announced, as she came out of the building with Dad and Jim.

"Hooray!" I cheered, standing up. I scratched Zobe's neck.

"Come on, Zobe," I said. "We're going home."